Fifty-Fifty
A Novel in Many Voices

Fifty-Fifty
A Novel in Many Voices

Robbie Clipper Sethi

SILICON PRESS
Summit, NJ 07901, USA

www.silicon-press.com

Silicon Press
25 Beverly Road
Summit, NJ 07901
USA

First Edition
Printing 9 8 7 6 5 4 3 2 1   Year 07 06 05 04 03

Library of Congress Cataloging-in-Publication Data

Sethi, Robbie Clipper
   Fifty-fifty : a novel in many voices / Robbie Clipper Sethi.-- 1st ed.
      p. cm.
   ISBN 0-929306-24-4
   1. East Indian American women--Fiction. 2. East Indian
Americans--Fiction. 3. Grandparent and child--Fiction. 4. New York
(N.Y.)--Fiction. 5. Grandmothers--Fiction. 6. California--Fiction. 7.
Sikhs--Fiction. 8. India--Fiction. I. Title.
   PS3569.E767 F45 2002
   813'.54--dc21

                                                     2002012085

Acknowledgments

Excerpts of *Fifty-Fifty* have appeared or will appear in the following publications: *U. S. 1 Summer Fiction Issue, Other Voices,* and *Screaming Monkeys* (Coffee House Press).

The poetry in "Three Sisters" is taken from "The Eve of St. Agnes" by John Keats.

I don't trust myself to remember all of the people who read all or part of this book, and I apologize for omitting any in this public acknowledgment of my gratitude for their help, perspectives, and time. I want to give special thanks to Debbie Lee Wesselmann, Hema Nair, and Tacey Rosolowsky, who read it early on and were generous with both encouragement and criticism. C. J. S. Wallia went above and beyond first reader as the developmental editor for this publication. Thanks to Mary Morse for her help with the dust jacket, Beverly Maximonis for her keen eye and artistry, and Richard Weems, for reading "Exile." Also Robi Weinreich, Bill Roome, and Charlie Wetherell. Kim, thanks for having faith in this one, and Narain, thanks for the faith, hard work, and opportunity.

The Family

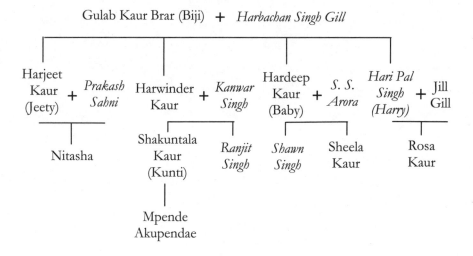

Gulab Kaur Brar (Biji) + *Harbachan Singh Gill*

Harjeet Kaur (Jeety) + *Prakash Sahni*

Harwinder Kaur + *Kanwar Singh*

Hardeep Kaur (Baby) + *S. S. Arora*

Hari Pal Singh (Harry) + Jill Gill

Nitasha

Shakuntala Kaur (Kunti)

Ranjit Singh

Shawn Singh

Sheela Kaur

Rosa Kaur

Mpende Akupendae

Males are shown in italics.

1 *Fifty - Fifty*

Rosa Kaur Gill
San Jose, California

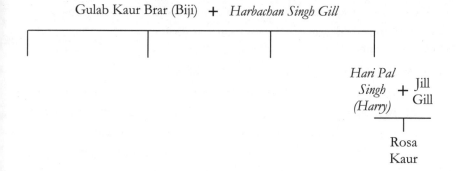

Gulab Kaur Brar (Biji) **+** *Harbachan Singh Gill*

Hari Pal Singh (Harry) **+** Jill Gill

Rosa Kaur

T HAT'S WHAT I call myself. My mother's a mongrel. That's
what *she* says: ancestors from so many different parts of Europe
that she can't tell *where* she got the same name as Dad's. It's true! It's
on her birth certificate—Gillian Ann Gill. As southern as the William
Williamses and Jo Ann Joneses of the West. I tease her: "If you'd hy-
phenated it, you'd be Jill Gill-Gill." Her light brown eyebrows come
together. Dad likes to say she got the best of Europe—height, pure
blue eyes, naturally blonde hair. She was one of those tall, beautiful
blondes that scare boys half to death. I'm like her. Except my hair is
brown; my eyes—I'm, like, a twelve-month tan. My grandmother tells
them, "Don't let Rosa stay out in the sun," or the Punjabi equivalent.
"She will turn black." So what do we do? We move to the eternal
sun—San Jose, California.

My father's Sikh. That has its *own* priorities: milk, meat, muscles.
Dad grew up in India, came for graduate school, met my mother, and
stayed. Then in Jersey he went through a mid-life crisis and quit Ortho to buy a Midas muffler franchise in California.

California, the promised land. Once New York was the end of
the rainbow. Then Dad got a job in the suburbs. That's where I was
born. New Jersey. It's a green place, in the summer anyway. We had
the whole side of a hill, trees, a little pond with crayfish and frogs.
And in the winter, ice. Then Dad saw the rainbow stretching clear
across the country and decided that the end with the pot of gold
must be on the other side.

I don't like it here in San Jose. I miss the snow. We drive up to
Tahoe and we ski, but it's not the same as waking up one morning
and getting a day off. As soon as I graduate I'm going back—
Princeton—Ivy League like my cousin Shawn. He's at Harvard. My
cousins Kunti and Nitasha went to Rutgers. Mom says if I have to go
to a state university, I might as well stay in California. Dad has his eye
on Stanford, just up the road. He wants me to be a genius, not to
change from the little girl I was in Jersey, look American, but don't
act too American. He hates it when I come right from school to

work, and his mechanics look out from the undersides of cars and call out, "Rosie! Hi! How's high school?"

"Dad's like, "You be careful who you talk to.""

"Dad! Those guys work for you. They're human."

"Do you have homework?"

"Homework?"

I *hate* my new school. I could teach sophomore English myself. I told my teacher, "Yeah. I *like* Judy Blume. I read all her stuff. When I was *twelve*. (Including *Wifey*, don't tell Dad!) But—I was expecting, maybe, *Scarlet Letter*? It's in video?"

The teacher's face got all red, like that letter on Hester Prynn's chest. "Your English is good. What kind of accent is that?"

"What accent?"

"We'll be reading 'Cinderella' next. You'll like that."

"Grimm?"

"Oh, no. I mean, it's uplifting. More than *Blubber*."

"I mean the German—get me out of here!" I leaned across the empty desk.

She shot back, hugging her roll book and that slim paperback, straight blond hair falling behind her shoulders. "You have to pass English to go on to junior year." It was almost a whisper.

Math was easier. And in New Jersey algebra had been my *worst*. Dad used to stand over me at the kitchen table. The glare of the tiffany lamp turned the paper blue. "This is simple. And important. Master maths and you can do anything—medicine, engineering . . ."

Mom understands me better. She pays cash for every A I get.

The girl next to me, her hair bleached as light an orange as she could probably get it, red nails four inches, couldn't follow long division. She gaped at the board, numbers piled up, blue on white, the latest in chalkboard technology. I asked her, "Haven't you ever subtracted the remainder before?"

I caught the teacher before she made it out the door. "I think I'm in under my head. I mean, I know it. Couldn't you get me into some math I can't do?"

The hall was filling up with bodies, rushing by like water through a pipe. "You'll have to speak to someone in the office."

I skipped lunch. The secretary was even busier than she had been when I'd enrolled myself in the summer. Mom was back in Jersey then, selling the house with its high, latticed windows, its tile kitchen and my big, light room with its own bath. If she knew that Dad let me walk to the school myself, on a day so cool and dry I couldn't believe it was summer, she'd have thrown a fit. But he was already working fifteen-hour days! Now that it was fall and school was in session, California was hot. Clerks and teachers milled around the secretary on the other side of a high counter. Students nudged my elbows, whined. I whined louder.

"You've got to stick with it, honey." She leans on the counter, dirty blond ponytail separating on the back of her neck. "It's only the first day." And she laughs, kind of loud and horsy.

"No. I need an upgrade. I do better."

"Sure you do. Your English is perfect."

"If my English is so perfect, why can't I get through?" And I thought about the kids who came in with only Spanish, Chinese.

I walked home. Couldn't stand to face another class. Mom was standing on the back of the couch hanging fully lined, brocade winter curtains from New Jersey. My grandmother, her dyed brown hair pulled back in a bun, sat on the couch in front of her leaning toward the television, on which a perfectly groomed male, blond hair moussed and jelled, spoke in low tones with a woman with cap-like, cream-colored hair. I slammed the door. "School is just too dumb! We're doing arithmetic in math, and English has us reading books I memorized in grade school."

"Didn't they put you in gifted and talented?" Mom looked down across our shimmery, white sofa. My grandmother said something. I was too upset to figure it out. Even my aunts, Dad's sisters, spoke Punjabi; then they criticized me when I couldn't speak it. But where would I have learned it? Mom went on: "Do they *have* gifted and talented?"

"The secretary didn't even ask. And I *gave* her my report cards."

Mom stepped onto the shiny floorboards and crossed the dining room into our cubicle-sized kitchen. "Dad should have gone over there with you," she said, picking up the phone.

"He was working on his golden touch. Besides, I'm five foot six, fifteen, reasonably intelligent, of sound mind and body—"

"You're growing up too fast." Then she told the school she'd had to pick me up for a doctor's appointment. She was sorry. She forgot she was supposed to tell the office in advance. She'd be happy to come in and explain it to the principal. The superintendent if he wasn't available.

They couldn't give her an appointment until Friday. By then I think I might have made an impression. "You're the best in the class." More than one teacher told me that. "Your parents must be proud."

Even the kids were impressed. "Hey, kid. You from Albuquerque or something?"

"No. I'm from New Jersey."

"New Jersey? That's in New York, right?"

It was the kids who told me that there *was* "gifted and talented." I'd been placed on the slowest, most remedial track. Julio told me, "That's why this stuff is boring." His hair and eyes are as dark as mine, his skin as tan. "Flipping burgers at the 'King is more in-ti-lec-tu-al."

"Why are we in here?" Ms. Haldemann was lecturing on values, what they are and how we so desperately need them.

Julio's like, "Why? These Mexicans. They don't speak English. Know what I'm saying?"

"What are you?"

"Chicano. You some kind of Cuban? *Hablo español?*"

"No. *Sprechen Sie Deutsch?*"

"What's that?"

"German."

"I knew you was a foreigner."

I took to the Mexicans. Always going on about something or other, laughing. Just like Dad's side of the family. When they're in a good mood. I wished I'd signed up for Spanish instead of my mother's German. But the Mexicans stick to themselves in that school. So do African-Americans, turning into larger groups in the hallways and the cafeteria.

There I stood, tray in hands, burrito losing heat, milk gaining it, right beneath my nose. Voices rose as one loud, long mumble-jumble. Where did I fit in? There were even tables of Asians—Chinese, Japanese, Korean, Vietnamese. I caught sight of a long, narrow table lined with girls in jeans, T-shirts, hair unpermed, uncolored, rings only in their earlobes. I took the path of least resistance.

"Hi. I'm Rosa Gill."

"Where you from?"

"New Jersey." They looked at each other. Green eyes, blue eyes, brown. "Are you all from California? Weren't any of you born out of state?"

"Lisa is from Indiana."

Must have been Lisa, fluffy blond hair, small, who jabbed the tall girl who had spoken in the ribs.

The girl with brown hair said, "My ancestors come from Jersey. Where did yours?"

"All over the world."

"Well, we don't have an all-over-the-world table. But the South Americans sit over there." Lisa pointed toward a table bubbling over with words I couldn't understand.

I told them what they wanted to know: "My father's Indian."

"Oh!"

The tall one goes, "You know Rajeev?"

"This is *only* my second day."

"Rajeev is Indian."

I stood identified. I looked around for faces of the color I'd been boiled down to and saw one table anchored by a Sikh, his topknot wrapped in a swatch of black cotton—what my cousin Shawn called a bubble, like the one my cousin Ranjit used to wear. I'd never seen one on my father, since he'd cut his hair even before he'd met my mother. I walked over and told them I was Rosa Gill.

Hands shot out European fashion. "Oh, Gulab, Gulabi," my name translated. "Where you from?"

"New Jersey."

"I have an uncle in New Jersey."

"Haven't seen you in class. What are you taking?"

When I told them I had Haldemann's English, Johnston's math, they laughed; brown hands slapped the table. "New Jersey schools must be as bad as Jersey air."

"What did you say your dad does? Auto mechanics?"

"Does your Mum work? Or is she in India?"

"My mother's not Indian."

"American?"

"Do you know Chitra?"

"*She's* half American."

Brown eyes searched for the fifty-fifty table.

I thought about my cousins in the San Fernando Valley. Hundred-percent. I wondered how long that bloodline would stay pure. We had driven down to L.A. for my aunt's annual brothers-and-sisters party. A disk jockey announced in Hindi soundtracks from the latest

Indian movies while my cousins danced. In my jeans and T-shirt I felt underdressed. Even the kids pranced around in wide, long trousers, pink, red, yellow and electric blue, matching tunics shining with embroidered beads. The girls, that is. The boys wore jeans like me or chinos like my mom and dad.

On the long drive home I asked my grandmother why she never gave me Indian clothes.

My mother said, "She used to bring *me* suits. They never fit—too short and wide. I didn't like any of them enough to wear them anyway. You want to look nice when you're going out."

"You don't look good in loose clothes anyway," my father said, his eyes on the most boring highway I have ever seen—parched brown fields on either side, towns that might have been more comfortable in the plains Dad and I had crossed on our drive across the country.

"Your father prefers the svelte look," my mother said.

"On you maybe," I said.

"Girls should dress like girls," he said. "Biji gives you skirts."

What everybody calls my grandmother. Sitting next to me in the back, she patted me on the thigh and said something in Punjabi I didn't understand.

"She says she's going to buy you a suit," my father said.

"Oh. Great," I go. "Thanks."

When we got a chance to tell Dad about Mom's appointment with the principal, he was furious. "It's those jeans you wear! You should wear skirts! Plaid! And pleated!"

"They don't have uniforms in American public schools," my mother said, passing him the shrimp. "They don't have dress code either."

"If I dressed the way you wanted," I told them, "*everyone* would laugh." I thought about the girls I'd eaten lunch with. I looked down at the pasta on my plate.

Biji said something, but Mom and I couldn't understand her, and Dad wasn't listening. He even passed her the shrimp, which she would never eat. She called it "insects." "Agh," she gagged.

"Did they see your report cards?" Dad asked. "Your test scores?"

"I'm not sure they can *read*." I twirled a forkful of spaghetti.

"I should have gone with you."

"You're never home."

He had no manager that he could trust, so how could he leave Midas even to argue with what *he* called the *headmaster* of the school that had placed me wrong? Mom had to argue on her own.

When I came home, she beckoned and pointed upstairs, where we always went when we wanted to talk without Biji interrupting. "Have I been promoted?" I go, flopping onto the king-sized bed, covered with a homemade patchwork quilt Mom picked up at the New Jersey State Fair.

"When you were a baby," she said, "people used to ask me how I'd managed to adopt you."

"Oh, God, you're not going to tell me they switched me in the hospital. I look exactly like Dad's sisters. Before they got fat."

"No, you're a Gill. On both sides." She joined me on the bed, stretching her long legs next to mine across the green and lilac patches. "I told *that* to your principal. He could hardly hide his disbelief. And I don't think it was the name. He even said, 'But you're American!'"

"Why is everybody in California so convinced that I'm a foreigner?" I asked.

"It occurred to me halfway through the conversation: they thought you were Mexican."

"Mexican?"

"We gave you a name both grandmothers could pronounce. Trouble is around here Rosa sounds Spanish. And you don't look Scottish enough to be a proper Gill."

"What does this have to do with 'tard English and math?'"

"'Tard?"

"As in *re*tard? Duh!"

"Oh, Rosa, that's as bad as putting down the Mexicans. Or Indians."

"Do I get out of it?"

"I'm quoting: 'You see, Mrs. Gill, that community is not in general interested in the school. Or education, for that matter.'"

"How can they be interested in school? They need every member of the family working in order to pay the rent."

"Dr. Floystrup told me, 'We try our best to instill the work ethic in all of our students. If they want college preparatory classes, they can sign up for them along with all of the rest of the students. It's because of them that we even *have* a vocational track.'"

"I didn't want to move here," I said. "I wanted to stay in Jersey."

Mom sat back on an Indian pillow studded with tiny mirrors and looked up at the ceiling. Sunlight pouring through the window hit the mirror work casting reflections on the smooth white ceiling, hundreds of flickering stars. "It reminds me of the school *I* went to," she said. "We were farmers. All of my sisters got good grades. We had to. My mother hung over our homework at the kitchen table every night."

"Like Dad. Before Midas."

"No matter how well we did—A's in English, B's in math and science—we *never* got into the honors classes—they called them honors classes then."

"God, did they think you were farmers, you didn't need to go to college?"

Mom shrugged. "When my sisters and I told the teachers we wanted to go, they suggested county colleges, state teachers colleges. Your aunt Lena went out of state, the University of Tennessee."

"Well," I said, "at least they weren't racist. Your uncle was a Nazi."

"Not an officer," she said, "and on the Russian front. But that's not the point. How did we get into that? As of tomorrow you go to Classics of English Literature."

"Yes!"

"And Trigonometry."

"Ouch!"

"There's a price to be paid for acknowledging that you are Asian."

But I'm not Asian. I find that out from Jenny Tanaka and Simon Chen in Trig. I'm not even Southeast Asian, like Joe Nguyen. They lump me in with Rajeev Patel, full-blooded, of such a different ethnic group from us Punjabis that my grandmother is always passing comments about Gujarati food, Gujarati clothing, "Gujarati!" she says. Rajeev's parents might call us pushy and materialistic. Even the white kids in the class, Peter Fradkin and Jennifer Miller, among others, can't believe that every new equation makes me break out in a sweat.

"Must be the European blood," I tell my father, "*Savoir faire, Sturm und Drang.*"

"Must be you're paying too much attention to dressing up and dances, not enough attention to your studies."

"That's bogus. Totally."

It kills him when I put on a pair of leggings and an exercise top and go back to school at night. But I can't even dance with Julio or Jamal without the Asians, Anglo-Saxons and Jews from Classics of

English Literature shouting in my ear above the drums and bass line, "Rosa! Why are you hanging out with *them*? Be *careful!* You're too young to have a baby!"

The difference between New Jersey and California, as I see it, is in California it's *in* to be a group. And the stereotypes are different. We have different Hispanics. But I don't have to live in groups that I do not believe in. I'm fifty-fifty. Only *half* Californian, and against my will. At least half easterner. *North*-easterner. Half intellectual. The other half likes the way that Julio calls me Indo-dweeb and urges me to dance: "Dance! Forget about what goes on in that pretty head of yours! People are people. All of us will one day be some kind of fifty-fifty. All of us will speak the same language. Spanglish."

"Punjablish."

Rajeev requests a record popular in England, and the Indian kids, like my cousins when they hear this stuff, go wild. "What the hell is this?" says Julio, and his hips stop swaying.

I show him how to stick his butt out, shift his feet and twist his hands up high. "It's the kind of music my father danced to. At weddings. In India. Before I was born."

"When do I meet this funky muffler man? I could use a job."

I laugh. I see this boy shouting "Rosie! Rosalita!" from beneath a chassis. Dad glares. But he doesn't need to worry. Julio and I can't *do* much more than dance. *His* family would *kill* him.

"Just wait till I ace Trig," I tell him. Get into Princeton and Dad might just stop worrying I'll turn out like my cousin Kunti, the single mother in the family, or her brother Ranjit, the addict. If King Midas lives to pay for it. By that time the east coast may be just as clannish. California is a trendsetter.

But I can never eat my lunch at just one table. I will always be fifty-fifty: what other people perceive me to be, and what I am. The best of both worlds. Me.

2 Third Generation

Rosa Kaur Gill
Half Moon Bay, California

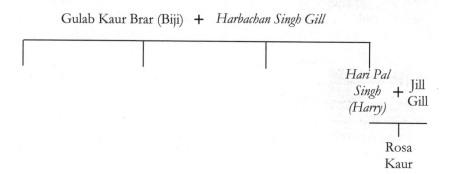

Gulab Kaur Brar (Biji) + *Harbachan Singh Gill*

Hari Pal Singh (Harry) + Jill Gill

Rosa Kaur

THIS IS A book about my family. Father's side. He calls me "third generation." As far as he's concerned, his mother's the first of a long line of women. He doesn't remember his grandmother. She died before he was born—of hepatitis. She got it after the locals threw her out of her home, in what is now Pakistan, and she and her husband and her sons had no other way to get to Delhi, the capital, than walk. Dad has three older sisters. In fifth grade I learned that he was "first generation" because he was born in India. He moved here when he was twenty-one. Even Biji's a first-generation immigrant—a permanent resident of the United States. In terms of immigration, I'm what they call "second generation," which is really weird because I'm the first kid in Dad's family to be born in the United States. That ought to make me "first generation," but then my father and grandmother would be "zero generation," or "zero" and "minus-one," and that makes about as much sense as "generation X" or "Generation Next" or any other label.

There's even a "fourth generation"—Biji's great-granddaughter and my second cousin, Mpende. (She's second-generation too, but this is getting confusing!) I don't know my cousins very well. They grew up all over the world, and even now they live so far away, we hardly see them.

That's not to say we don't keep in touch. My grandmother calls each of my aunts and cousins every day and fills my father in on the news. Most of the time she lives with us. But at least once a year she goes to visit my youngest aunt in England. From there it's an eight-hour flight to Africa. She stays in Kenya with her middle daughter, though she hates that place. It's a five-hour flight from Nairobi to India, where my father's oldest sister lives. So the family is together. But not in the way my grandmother wanted it to be.

She raised my aunts with the idea that no matter who they married, they would always be closer to each other than anybody else. So like the *Three Sisters* in a play I read in high school—World Literature—my three aunts are always whining about having to live where their husbands' jobs are. They want to be within walking distance of each other. Except that instead of Moscow, America's the place they pine for—a destination arrived at after years of trial and error. For my grandmother and aunts, the concept of growing up and living in your own house with only your spouse and kids—maybe a dog or cat—is, simply put, foreign. The plan was: send the boy in the family to America. My grandmother and any unmarried grandchildren could live with him. My aunts began sending their kids to Rutgers because me and my father and mother were living in New Jersey at the time. They thought my mother and father would make sure my cousins studied and stayed away from foreigners—meaning Americans, like me. The kids were expected to get a job near us, get married—again, near us—and then my aunts would come over and we'd all live together.

Nitasha is the oldest of my generation and the first of my cousins to come to the United States. She was born in India in 1970, which my mother says was "one helluva year." Mom didn't know my father then. She was in college in New York. He was still in India.

I asked Nitasha how she got a Russian name. She said it was fashionable in India at the time. According to my aunt Jeety, Nitasha's mother, in the Middle East, where she lived when she was first married to Uncle Prakash, she had a Russian doctor, who was very nice, and she had always liked Russian names. I asked her why she spells it with an i, and she just looked at me, as if there wasn't any other way to spell it.

'Tasha, as we kids shorten it, might have been the first to come over, but she was the last to shock the family with a story that questions the way my grandmother and even my aunts think about love and marriage. My cousin Kunti was the first to make the family tabloids. It was because of Kunti that my mother made me carry condoms in my purse. But I think there's a lot more to it than the "girl in trouble" of my mother's generation.

Kunti was born in 1973, in India because her mother, my father's middle sister—the only sister everybody calls, for some reason, by her full name, Harwinder—was visiting my grandmother in Delhi. In India daughters go back to their parents' houses to have their babies.

Kunti is short for Shakuntala. It's a Sanskrit name. I read *that* play on my own. It's about a girl who got pregnant by some king, and just like President Clinton and a bunch of actors, rock stars, and athletes today, the king said not only did he not father the child, he didn't even have sex with the girl. They didn't have DNA in those days. But they *did* have the gods, and the gods took care of Shakuntala until the king came to his senses and remembered—"Oh, yeah, *that* Shakun-tala!" Kunti's the name of another Indian heroine. I read about her too. Kunti was able to call down the gods herself. But when she called them, all they wanted was to have sex with her. She got a few babies out of that. My cousin Kunti is the only one of my generation who has a kid. She gave her daughter a Swahili name, I think in pro-test of her mother giving her such a long Sanskrit one.

Sheela's the cousin closest to my age. But even *she's* three years older. She has a name that works in both cultures. She was born in England. But just like Nitasha, she spells it her own way. Punjabi does not have an i e, before or after c! Sheela's mother—everybody calls her Baby, do you believe it?—is my father's youngest sister. She got tired of waiting for her kids to be old enough to join Nitasha and Kunti for college, so she sent them to America for high school. Why she sent them to her husband's family in California instead of us—still in New Jersey at that time—I will never understand. Maybe it was the reputation that pulled my father out to California a few years later. Knowing what I know now about California high schools, I would have to ask, "What was she thinking?" But I'll let Sheela and her brother Shawn tackle that one.

Because Sheela's so much younger, her story comes after her cousins and her brother already defied tradition. Not that *that* made it any easier for her.

My two boy cousins—Kunti's younger brother, Ranjit, and Sheela's older, Shawn, didn't make it easier for anyone! Both were born in 1979. Shawn changed the spelling of his name from Shaan to Sean in England; then when he came to America, he signed it Shawn. Kunti's brother scored the most prestigious name in the family— Ranjit Singh, after the most famous Sikh king. I've never met him. I've heard stories though. And I've seen pictures. Ranjit's face is stuck in my head, the way I close my eyes and see Keanu Reeves for days after I've watched one of his movies. Ranjit and Shawn used to be what Indians call "fast friends." In Europe instead of discovering the civilization England thought it was bringing to India, Ranjit discovered a troupe of heroin addicts nicer than anyone he'd ever met. He came here to live with his sister, but he didn't find the same spirit of cooperation in the streets of New Brunswick, New Jersey, so he left. No one knows where he is, but I imagine if he told his story, he would start with the trip he took with Shawn, long before he came to the United States. Shawn's story starts a little bit later.

I think the reason the family lives so far apart might have something to do with what happened to my grandmother, grandfather and aunts in 1947. When the British left India, they drew a border to create a new country, Pakistan, right where my grandparents were living at the time. They're Sikhs, a religion established about five hundred years ago. Over the years, Sikhs came into conflict with Muslims, though my grandmother says that Sikhs and Muslims lived very comfortably side-by-side before the politicians created a country where Sikhs and Hindus were no longer welcome. My grandparents had to get out and fast. They left everything. My grandmother was almost thirty when she had to start over, with three daughters and no place to live.

The first time she rode with us from San Jose to Los Angeles—a long drive down the central valley of California—she looked out over the miles and miles of furrowed flat fields and burst out crying. She tried to tell me about her childhood. But I think her memories are all bundled up in her head in Punjabi, the language of her parents. She's more comfortable speaking it than English, though she understands TV enough to follow the soaps. Dad tried to help her out by telling me bits and pieces—how my grandparents and aunts got out by plane, which spared them the danger of traveling on trains. Whole trains full of people were killed. But Dad got it only secondhand himself. He was born in Delhi. In a house my grandmother built. That is, she sold her gold to build it.

If I want to hear my grandmother's story in the way it was meant to be told, I will have to learn Punjabi. And I will. As soon as I start college. Until then I'll let her tell it as best she can, as she remembers it, and as it happened.

3   Exile

Gulab Kaur Gill
Half Moon Bay, California

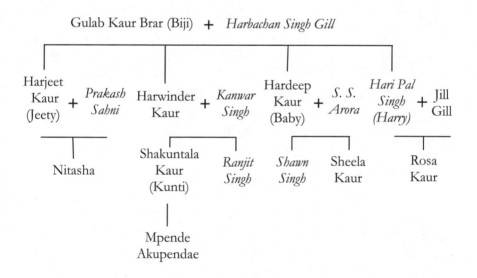

Gulab Kaur Brar (Biji)   **+**   *Harbachan Singh Gill*

Harjeet Kaur (Jeety)   **+**   *Prakash Sahni*

Harwinder Kaur   **+**   *Kanwar Singh*

Hardeep Kaur (Baby)   **+**   *S. S. Arora*

Hari Pal Singh (Harry)   **+**   Jill Gill

Nitasha

Shakuntala Kaur (Kunti)   *Ranjit Singh*

Shawn Singh   Sheela Kaur

Rosa Kaur

Mpende Akupendae

I HAVE TRIED to tell this story to my granddaughter, Rosa. She has my own name, in English because her mother is not even Indian. My daughter-in-law cannot speak my language, and for that reason, my Rosa did not grow up speaking it, like my grandchildren in India and Africa. But my English is not good for things that come out sounding just the way I want to say them in my own Punjabi. So you must imagine that you understand the language of my father's rich, warm earth, the way I wish the daughter of my only son could understand me when I remember the stories I would like her to know.

When I was a girl the family had everything. All the land beneath the cotton, corn and cane that brought our family wealth—apples from Kulu, silks, the gold our mother gave us when we married— that belonged to my father. Every morning before any of us children were awake, he was gone. To the fields, the village. But unlike my son, in this America, where everybody works, works, works, my father came home, always, to the family before the sun would set. A crowd of servants, villagers and dogs always followed, his white turban gleaming in the sun, black beard open on the starched, white shirt stretched tight across his chest. "Where is my little rose?" I can still hear his deep, warm voice. On our wide, marble veranda, shaded with bougainvillea, he would always make a space for me, his favorite of all the girls. And I would listen as our villagers squatted on the hard, packed earth in front of our house to hear my father speak: *that grain that will not sprout, soak every seed in holy water from our Gurdwara; that daughter-in-law who will not stop crying for her father's house, you must love your sons' wives, love them, as if they were your own, good daughters.*

We believe that creatures pass through many lives. Every animal must be reborn into a different body. I have lived through countless of these lives. Still in this same, tired flesh.

Whole day I sit in my son's house in this California, in what these Americans call a family room. Only family I see is on TV—loud and disrespectful, in a language I have never spoken half as well as I can understand. My son does not come home until the night, and even then he has nothing to say, he and that American he married. Even my own granddaughter will not sit with me before she runs to her own private room. "Homework, Biji!"

Is there something that does not please God that He must fling the children of one small, weak woman to the very edges of this earth? Sometimes lying on a plastic cot outside of the closed-up, air-conditioned house, I shut my eyes, and I can almost smell the dung smoke rising from the flat-flat plains, hear the voices of my father, mother, sisters and brothers filling up the house that I will never see again. As if the marriage that took me from my father's village was not exile enough!

I could not disobey my father. Tears came to my eyes like the streams that cut the earth during the monsoons. My father had found a good family, an educated boy, and before I could even think about it, it was time. I looked up through the red-red veil that covered my head and saw for the first time the father of those children I would one day have.

In the bed of Harbachan Singh Gill, my childhood died. Only in my pregnancy could I go back to my father's house. And after each daughter was born, I went back to the field, where no one working for the chief engineer in charge of roads and bridges dared to look with pity on Gulab Kaur Gill because she had not had a son.

It was in one of those large, brick houses we moved in and out of while my husband worked on one site or another that all of the life I knew changed so much that I can only call it death. Blood poured at the very mention of a Muslim Punjab. Servants whispered in the courtyard. Hindus took their wages and disappeared. We dismissed the Muslims. Bodies turned up in the streets, shouts rang out both day and night, fires took the homes of our neighbors. Shortages of rice, bread, even milk grew worse as people hoarded, hoping to survive inside their homes. One day our old servant pounded at the door we now kept locked. "For the children," he said, lowering a brass pot from the ragged cloth wrapped around his head. "Why should they drink water when the cows still give?"

Tears blinded me as I carried his pot through the many rooms of that house, to the courtyard, out through the gate into the garden, where I poured his milk onto the damp, monsoon-soaked earth. Harwinder, my middle daughter, pulled on the bright cottons I always wore in that place and cried. My first-born, Jeety's eyes widened like the eyes of owls. I returned the empty vessel and gave the man who once had been our servant, almost a member of the family, a coin.

Whole day I put clothing, the children's toys, into bags and bundles. When my husband finally came home, I told him, "He was a good boy. The children loved him. But how can we be sure his Muslim friends have not poisoned the milk? At least you must let me take the children to my father's farm, where cows and chickens—"

"The border will cut right through your father's house. On one side Muslims will be slaughtered; on the other, Hindus, Sikhs. Wear all of your gold beneath your clothing, as much clothing as you can. Government is sending me to Delhi."

"What will happen to my mother-father?"

"Your mother-father are your brothers' responsibility," he said. "It is all I can do to get *my own* family out."

We met his mother, his brothers and their wives and children, even his sisters and their families at the airfield. I had not known my husband was such an important man. Either that or he had paid such a bribe to get a plane to exile all of us from our proper homes.

In Delhi, sleeping arm to arm—with three small children—on the concrete floor of a two-room flat with my husband's brothers' wives, all of their naughty children, my husband's mother and the mother and children of the man who rented the flat, himself sleeping on the other side of the room beside his father, my husband and my husband's brothers, I fell sick with worry. We heard nothing of my mother-father, brothers or sisters and their families. For all we knew they were dead—slaughtered by Muslim mobs, starved. Then we heard from friends: "I saw them. Your father and your mother." Or "I was on a train with your sister." And one cold morning I heard my father's name—"Hazar Singh! It is our own Hazar Singh Brar!"—and I ran out to the street. Dogs prowled sniffing in the garbage in the dust, cows behind them. And there was my father, his white cottons brown with dirt, his beard completely white, leaning on a stick. I fell into his arms. "How did you get here?" I shouted. "Who brought you? I will give him all my gold!"

"God gave me feet," he said. "What would God do with your gold?"

I wept. Wealthiest landowner in all of the Punjab, and he had to walk, all of my family walked, all the way to Delhi. For the rest of their lives my mother-father lived with my brothers in a small-small flat in the vegetable market. I stayed with my husband and his family, scrubbing every day, I, the daughter of a landlord. Because the sweeper came only once a day, and no one else would clean. And all I heard for my trouble was, "Who are you to come into our flat and tell us how to live? You yourself are stinking the toilet, you and your three daughters."

When I wanted to talk to my husband, I had to wait until he came home for the night. Then I had to stay awake until everyone was sleeping and crawl to the men's side of the room, taking care not to step on the women, children, and men who lay between us. But I could never talk without someone interrupting, no matter how late in the night. Kneeling on that hard-hard floor, I heard my mother-in-law, "Why must you disturb my son? He will get a big house for all of the Gill brothers. Wait and see."

I was the one who had arranged those brothers' marriages, so many families did I know from my father's village and the villages where my husband and I lived. It was how I earned respect in my mother-in-law's house. But as good as those girls were, as grateful as my husband's brothers, I could not live with them. After I had joined my husband in the field, I grew used to keeping a house of my own, rooms for anyone who came to stay, quarters for the servants, gardens.

What to do? I covered my head and went out while my husband was at work, intent, as he was, on feeding a family on the salary of a civil servant. There I stood, alone in the dusty street, the smell of diesel making me long for the dung smoke of my home, my littlest, whom we called Baby, in my arms, the folds of one leg of my *salwars* bunched up in Jeety's little fist, my free hand stuck to Harwinder's sweaty fingers. Women in cheap cotton saris balanced baskets of wet cement on their heads, the muscles on their strong, black necks standing out like the roots of banyan trees. In another life, I might have been as poor as these girls, as black, my children playing in the dust. Men in tattered cotton piled bricks into walls, smoked cigarettes, shouted: "Eh! Water!" Their children had all stopped fetching to stare at me and my three girls.

"I want a house!" I shouted.

One of the men laughed, long and cruel.

"It need not be big. On that plot, there." I let go of Harwinder's hand. She wailed and pulled my salwar against my calf.

He walked away.

"I will pay you cash."

"Everyone is giving cash."

Even his children laughed at the daughter of a respected land-owner standing in a city street begging for a house. But I would not walk away. Where was I to go? I could feel my own face burning in the sun, I stood so long waiting-waiting, the children crying-crying. He did not even look in my direction when he said, "If you buy me bricks enough for walls, I will build your *not too large* bungalow."

I took my gold, the gold that showed the world how rich my husband's family was supposed to be, and sold it to the jeweler willing to pay the most.

If my husband felt humiliated by my naked wrists, he could buy me another set of pure gold bangles. "Why must you be so impatient?" He tried not to shout. His entire family sat around us in the crowded flat.

"See how my daughter-in-law cares for the family," my mother-in-law boasted. So my husband could not say another word. And how was it so strange? All over the city wives were selling their marriage gold to put roofs over their families' heads.

In that house another life began. Same tired flesh. But not so tired that it could not bear the son my husband wanted. For this birth there was no father's house to return to. My mother did not even live to see my son, and my husband was so afraid that I would lose the child if I knew how sick my mother was, he would not let me see her. But I knew. I saw her. I was not so weak as to lose my only son, though I lost my mother, and all because of some stupid politicians.

No crowds of villagers turned out to bless the long-awaited grandson of Hazar Singh Brar. Only the family and friends who had settled in New Delhi, the clothing they had worn out of the Punjab fading on their backs. My husband, silly with joy, took a taxi to Old Delhi and rounded up three *hijras*, the men who dress like women. How he smiled, his fair face red, though my mother's ashes had only just sunk beneath the surface of the Ganges, as the eunuchs clicked their cymbals and jingle-jangled their glass bracelets on the street in front of our veranda.

We named him Hari Pal Singh, because, as for all my children, the holy book fell open on the name of God. He was my father's favorite. He was naughty, active, would not listen, even to my father. "I can give him nothing," my father said. "You and Harbachan must send him to the best school in this city, so that he may take his place among the wealthy and important."

I obeyed my father, as always. But I must say. This education may have given my son the opportunity to study in the United States. It may have prepared him for a job in one of the top pharmaceutical companies in the world. But it will never make him the man my father was. Hari gave up that important job and bought a stinking, smelling, car-repair shop, a business good enough for my husband's sisters' children, who could not succeed in college, let alone obtain a PhD. He may have bought a big house, in this California, where the winters are not so cruel as the winters in New York or New Jersey, places where my son has lived. But he has no family. Just one daughter, who will leave as soon as she gets married. Girls must always leave the family. Only a son can provide for his parents when the father is old.

No one stops by, the way that family and friends always sat together in my house in Delhi. I sit alone, the sky dark before my son brings the family home. My daughters live across the world, no matter where I stay, their daughters clear across this cold country.

All of my life I have only tried to keep the family together. I found good boys for my daughters; I was always the best at finding boys. But my naughty girls! First family I invited were rich Punjabi Sikhs, their eldest son in a bright pink turban so tight it pulled his eyes into the slants of the Chinese, who we were at war with at the time. "Come in, come in," I said, and they sat in my drawing room, on the red velvet divan, mother, father, and son, even the boy's sisters, his little brother, hairs just sprouting on his smooth fair cheeks. "Where is Jeety?" I shouted. "Have her bring the tea!" I had left my silver tea set and the thin China cups on the counter in the kitchen.

My own smooth-faced son got up to fetch his sister, the first of my daughters to turn twenty. Jeety had grown up beautiful with straight brown hair, braided to the backs of her knees, large gray eyes, the pale complexion my father had passed down to all of us.

We kept a goat in the alley. My son had never been able to drink cows' milk. And it was that goat that my naughty daughters led into the drawing room, Jeety's sheer magenta *chunni* draped over its ugly horns.

The boy's mother stood up. "Have you no shame!"

Harwinder, who should have been more intelligent, on one side of that goat, and Baby, who should have shown more respect, were laughing so hard they could not stand. I gave them each a slap. Tears ran down their cheeks. The boy's family rushed out onto the street, shouting, my husband after them, trying to explain. What could be explained?

Baby said, "The family doesn't want a girl who works."

"Jeety doesn't want to quit the Cottage Industries Emporium," Harwinder said.

What could I do? Even if a family would allow her to work, all of the money would go to them. And how was I to part with her? She had been my favorite, I will admit, the gentlest of all my girls. How I had wept at the very thought of leaving my father's house! But a girl without a husband is a girl who will never have children, and what kind of future can a woman have if she has no son to care for her and light her funeral pyre?

Years went by, and finally Jeety grew bored selling the block printed silks and homespun cottons she had bought on discount for all of my girls. But every year more and more of our suitable boys were taken. Or there was something wrong—boys who could not make a living, smelled like alcohol, or had affairs. Then one family came all the way from the Middle East, where so many Indian boys had gone to make money off the rich Arabs. My father did not approve: "He is not even a Sikh, let alone a Jat. Yes, the family is rich.

But he is the youngest." But how were we to get a Sikh at this late date, let alone a first-born son, who would assure my daughter the most respect in a Hindu family? It was 1963. No one in the city married girls to boys that they had never seen. And Jeety fell in love with Prakash Kumar Sahni's cut brown hair and clean-shaven face. They looked like film stars, my beautiful daughter and this handsome boy. Even my husband agreed.

I did not know how hard it would be to live through this, my daughter's exile. Every evening, long after the sun had set, I sat on a rope cot on the veranda. Girls swayed their long, heavy hair, passing by, so much like my daughter I would jump, suddenly remember where she was and cry. What to do? With one daughter settled in the Middle East, what could I do but move the whole family there? Jeety's letters bragged about the good things she had bought— overstuffed divans, Persian carpets, thick, velvet draperies to keep out the sun. There were many Indians in that place. Every night they went to parties. I had never lived by the sea. And I did not ever care to. But for some reason the first time I looked out on that stretch of blue, nothing between the balcony of Jeety's flat and the line of sky across the water, I remembered the flat-flat fields my father had once walked, as far as the eye could see. And I promised myself that before my father breathed his last, I would reclaim as much of this world as I could for my children.

On that first visit, I had brought Harwinder. She had nothing in India, nothing, crying-crying, swearing she would kill herself if I did not send her to the university. "Do you want me out of Delhi?" she said. "Fine. Send me to London."

"London?" I said. "What is in London?"

"Shelley," she said. "Keats."

"What are these Shelleys and Keatses that you must abandon your family for them?"

My middle daughter was intelligent, no doubt. I would have allowed Jeety to pay her fees in a practical course of study, like medicine or engineering. But what sense did it make for her to ruin her eyes before I could find her a boy who could bear to marry a girl who was always reading-reading? One of Prakash's friends would have to turn my daughter's head away from those books I always took from her. I could see them watching; it was only a matter of time before Harwinder rose her tiny eyes and looked back.

We do not believe in love as a way of matching girls and boys. Love may draw a boy and girl together, it is true, but after the first few months of passion, what is left unless the boy and girl are as well matched as coriander and cumin? But my daughters had such minds of their own, what was I to do? If the boy was good, his family rich, we could have no objection.

I cannot say I liked the boy my daughter chose. The family was good, that was not a problem, with a big house in Nairobi, Kenya, Africa, where Kanwar Singh, even his father, had been born. He had no brothers to dispute his inheritance, and so much money that he could have gone to college anywhere—India, England, even America. But he had not wanted education. That was a problem. While we had been trying to persuade the most intelligent girl in the family to forget English poetry and marry a good boy, Kanwar's widowed mother had been promising him anything if he would only finish a degree. Instead he left his mother in Nairobi and started an import-export business across the sea. What had my daughter ever loved in him? He was a handsome Sikh. That was certain, with a thick, black beard and deep, brown eyes. Harwinder blushed and giggled when he came into the flat, so much so that Jeety had to speak for her sister. When this Kanwar let her speak at all. The boy sat on Jeety's brocade divan, his long legs in tight, shiny trousers spread into a V, bragging: "Business is going well, profits over a million; mother is happy. How could she not be happy in a house of ten-twelve rooms, surrounded by gardens? Only last week I ordered a Thunderbird direct from this Ford Motor Company in America."

After this marriage took another daughter, I thought, what could be so bad, moving the whole family to a city on the sea, even if it was a foreign city? No one in the family lived as well, and my daughters could easily find a husband for their sister. Then, in three-four years, after Hari finished his degree, they could find a job and a wife for him there. We would all live together on that stretch of sea and sky. It was not the Punjab—ringing with the music of our mother tongue, the great turbans of our farmers looming in the sun—and my poor father would not live to see us settled. But we could be wealthy in the Middle East. It was rich, and all of the children would be together.

What are the chances that a family may be forced out twice in one life? My daughters' letters filled with worry: *If the Communists nationalize the businesses, Kanwar and Prakash will not make money. What are we to do?*

How was I to send my Baby? It was only a matter of time before I got the call: Jeety and Prakash were in Bombay, in Prakash's family house. They were fine. They had even managed to sell the furniture and convert the currency to gold.

"Where is your sister?" I asked, weeping for my daughters.

"Harwinder is better off than me! She has a big house in Nairobi, with only her mother-in-law. They have put us in one small-small room with no place for anything."

All I heard was *Africa*. And I had to go, all the way across the Arabian Sea, to bear this exile of my middle daughter.

India was bad, so many beggars, cows in the city streets. But this Nairobi was the worst place I had ever seen. Men blacker than the blackest stone that comes out of the earth walked the streets in nothing more than rags, their legs rubbed red with the blood-red soil of that dusty place. Women showed their reddened black legs too, their hair so thick they have to braid each strand into a fringe so that it will not stand out on their heads like brushes. When a large blackie stopped Kanwar's Thunderbird at an iron gate in a high brick wall, I thought my heart would fail.

"He is our guard," Harwinder said, taking my hand away from my chest and squeezing it.

Kanwar drove up to a large, brick house, verandas all around, flowers of every color in the garden. It was good, Jeety was right about that, with empty rooms where no one ever slept, full of furniture, surrounded by grass clipped in the style of the British, who quit Africa ten, fifteen years after quitting India. But outside the window of the room in which I slept—alone, for the first time in my life, afraid all night that something would come in and kill me—all manner of strange animals cried out louder than the cars and buses of Delhi. And in the day, at teatime, we had to watch so that baboons would not steal the sugar.

Harwinder's mother-in-law was not bad, that much I could say. I tried to console, but Harwinder could not forgive meek, soft-spoken Rajindra Kaur for taking Kanwar's side. "She will never let me speak. She thinks he will stop if he thinks he has won."

"Taking a son's side may be natural in a mother," I said. "More important is the side a husband takes—his mother or his wife."

"Mummy never argues. Only cries. As if he has raised his hand to *her*."

This son-in-law was bad. There was no doubt. A woman might get used to her husband coming home so late she hardly ever sees him. I had. But there must be someone in the house. Kanwar's mother, for all of her mildness, could provide no company. And when Kanwar was at home, he gave no peace. He had taken to drinking more and more in Nairobi, where everybody drinks. There was nothing else to do. The British started it, with their clubs and toddies, out of idleness, just as they had ruined India. And when Kanwar drank too much, he shouted. He even shouted at me: "Do you know what this girl wants? She wants me to take her to England. Why? To become an Englishman? Like those poets you allowed her to moon over day and night!"

"You are ignorant," she said, so boiled up that she could not control her anger. But that was her nature. We were used to it.

Kanwar dared not raise a hand with his wife's mother in the house, but I could see the fire in his eyes, fed with alcohol the way a priest will feed a pyre with holy oil, and I was afraid for my daughter. What could I do? Take her to India and the scandal would follow us, even if Kanwar did not. Her father would never forgive me for taking her out of India in the first place. And who could keep this girl? One day soon my husband would retire, and inflation had already gobbled up his pension. Harwinder might get a job teaching English, all that she could do in Africa, but there were so many more teachers in India, and teaching English poetry had never made anyone rich, white or brown. All I had ever wanted for my daughters was the wealth that I had lost when I was forced to move to Delhi. Kanwar made a lot of money, in spite of his bad habits. What could I do but pass down to my daughter the wisdom of my own mother: "You must have a son. When he has a son, he may appreciate you, and you will have someone to love."

Indians lived well in Kenya, I could say that too, rich enough to buy anything they might be able to find in that poor place, and good luck finding it. We went to a party every night, and everyone dressed better than they dressed in India—saris and silk suits on the ladies, silk shirts on the men. But Indians had lived even better in Uganda. Everyone in Kenya told me that. Indians owned all the businesses, even the mint, where they made Ugandan money. Still they had been forced to leave, their million shilling businesses and mansions left to blackies, who had not had anything until the British brought the Indians to run their railroad. I could not allow some crazy man to force my Harwinder out—or her crazy husband to force her to stay until they would be thrown out—for the third time in her life. I had to get her out, with or without her husband. What kind of mother was I if I could not save my child from her fate? "I will send your brother to America," I promised her.

We were sitting in the sun on the second-floor veranda, drinking tea, as we always drank that strong, Kenyan tea, while Rajindra slept and Kanwar finished up at his office in the town. Strange birds cried from the avocado trees; beneath them a gardener, black as the African night, raked the fruit from the short clipped grass.

"America is too far," Harwinder said. "Why can't you send him to London?"

"England is finished," I said. "If they could not hold onto this place, what can an Indian get there? Everyone is saying that America is safe. No one gets kicked out. Borders are not drawn through people's lands. Americans are rich. I have seen them! Hippies giving rupees to our beggars, as if their god cares if they come back as cows or pariah dogs in that dusty city where I had to raise you girls."

I blamed exile for my daughters' city ways. Had they only grown up like me, in the house of a landlord, I would have found three strong Sikh farmers for them, rich families with land, gold.

Even the youngest of my three girls left me. How was she to stay? She would not agree to any boy I found for her, and it was difficult to find her any boy. Aunts and cousins gossiped: they had seen her going into the cinema with this boy, coming out of a coffeehouse with that boy. "Who are these boys?" I asked her. "If any one of them is suitable we will arrange a marriage."

Sometimes she laughed; sometimes she cried. She was the maddest of my daughters. On one of her visits, Harwinder said, "Better let me take Baby back. She has nothing here. And besides. How can I go without someone to protect me?"

What could I do? I could not send Harwinder back without someone to shame Kanwar into leaving her alone. The family was not so well connected in those days as to find my Baby a husband settled in America. The best Harwinder could do was a Nairobi Indian settled in London. Not a Jat. His hair cut, like Prakash's and his beard shaved off. But those things were no longer possible for the family. It took some time, but this daughter with the worst husband in the family made the best match for her sister. Suraj Singh Arora had been in the hotel business, but he got out of that and went back to accounting for a big multinational corporation. I was with them in London, a year after their marriage and not two months after Shawn, their first child, a son, had been born; I called America and told Hari to send me a ticket.

I did not recognize my own child. I was pushing my luggage, which I myself had lifted into a sturdy, steel wire cart, through a pair of swinging doors into the airport lobby. A tall, smooth-faced man bent in front of me and touched my feet. I shrieked.

"Biji? Are you sick?" He grabbed my arms.

"Ai-ya!" What could I do? I pulled him to my chest. "Who is this foreigner?" I said. "I left a proud Sikh with a sharp Punjabi turban and a full, black beard at the airport in New Delhi!"

"Biji," he said, "without you to starch my turbans—"

I should not have sent him so far away, I knew, without at least one of his sisters. He shaved his beard to be more like these Americans, I figured that out on my own, as he pushed my luggage through the doors to the taxi stand outside. They looked like girls, some of these Americans, their girls as tall and flat-chested as boys. Hari's clean face brought back the innocent round face of the son I had given birth to, and I wept, sitting next to the luggage that would not fit in the boot of the taxi, until the lights of the tallest buildings I had ever seen cleared before my eyes.

The wealth of America should not have surprised me. But the pictures I had seen had not prepared me for those steel towers, rising up into the sky like man-made Himalayas. My son lived all by himself in one of them. Everything was locked up, windows, doors. "It is for the cold," my son said. "You can take off your shawl. Inside the air is warm."

The tiny streets below felt like tunnels into which I had been dropped from a brighter world. My son bought me a coat, but it was so heavy that I could not wear it. In Kashmir, they weave the warmest wool that you can buy, so light that a whole shawl can pass through a ring, but no wool is a match for the wind that blows through New York streets. I spent all day, every day inside the flat.

I was only in America for two-three days before I saw that my son had not given up *all* of his habits. He did not get up in the morning, even when I called him two-three times. He could take a shower any time of day, he said, the water never went off. He had no classes in the morning, but as soon as I gave him breakfast, he went out. "To the university," he said. "I'll call you if I can't come home." Sometimes he did, and then I was left alone, only the television to keep me company until he came home, just like his father, in the night.

"Where are your friends?" I asked. No one ever stopped by, no one called. "Are you ashamed of your mother that you cannot call your friends for dinner, at least tea? I will make them chicken . . ."

I felt sorry for his friends, Indian boys, mostly, none of them married. I could have matched them all, so many families had I talked to looking for the best girl for my son, but so many of these boys were Gujaratis, Sindhis, Bengalis, even Madrasis, and one Muslim. In London all of Baby's friends had been Punjabis, even Harwinder's friends in Africa. Hari even knew some girls, Americans. I would have been suspicious if my son had not assured me that these girls were only friends, even one girl who made much of her family name sounding the same as ours, as if that could darken her colorless hair, like the hair of an old person, or shrink her to a decent size for a woman. This girl, Jill, started coming by so often that I had to warn my son, "Child, it may be dangerous to spend so much time with these girls. Indians may talk, and a family may not look well on you if they think you have girlfriends in America."

Hari's new, smooth face glowed red. "Why are you worried about that now?" he said. "I'm not ready to get married."

"Yes, but when you—"

"How can I get married? I don't even have a job. It could be years before I'm in a position to get married."

I comforted my daughters by reminding them that in America no one's land could be taken. We were not Red Indians that we could not live amongst the whites; in India Punjabis had lived beside the English for a hundred years. And in America these English were everywhere; I could tell by their white hair and gray-pink faces. India had never fought these Americans in any war. Americans would never let the Communists take over or send us to a country we had never seen. In America—I had heard this all my life—a poor man could be rich. He had only to work, and Sikhs were the hardest workers in the world.

I was back in India by the time my son got a job with the biggest pharmaceutical company in the world. What could I do? These Americans will not let an Indian stay for more than eight, ten months, and if I had not gone, I might not have been allowed to return. While I was waiting for my son to settle, grandchildren were born—first Jeety's Nitasha; then Harwinder's daughter, some Shakuntala or some such Sanskrit name. I should be glad she did not name her Agnes or Cristabel. Years passed before Harwinder had that son who was supposed to protect her from her husband. At least she gave him a good Sikh name—Ranjit. At the same time Baby had her first child, Shawn. I was there again, just after Baby's second child, a daughter, had been born, in her cold, dark flat in London, when she asked me, "Did Hari ever introduce you to a girl? Jill, her last name the same as ours. Isn't that funny? When you were with him, three years ago, in New York?"

I knew what she meant, but I could not admit it. "I met many girls. Boys too. Who is to say which one might have claimed our name?"

She bounced Sheela on her chest, patting her tiny back to stop her crying. "Hari says you know her. He says he would like to bring her to India."

"Why bring a girl to India? There are many girls in India."

"Biji, I think we will have to let him marry this girl. He has known her for three-four years. I think they might already be married."

It all fit together: the lack of roommates, the long hours he spent outside of the flat, the jokes about her name, the way that he was always passing hints that I should go back and take care of his father. He did not have the money to send his father a ticket, but he worried about him in India all alone. He would miss me, he said, but he would feel better about his father as soon as I went back.

I wept to think that I had lost my son and right under my nose. Right then I decided: I *had* to quit India. Everyone I knew had helped me find a lady doctor who was willing to marry a boy in America. I could not show my face, I, who had once been known as the best at arranging marriages. And I knew I had to accept the American wife because America *had* to have her price.

This country continues to exact a fee. It takes ten, fifteen years for these Americans to let a boy's real sister into the country. While my daughters waited for Hari to become a citizen, to sponsor them for immigration, they took care to educate their children in the best of English schools—in Bombay, Nairobi and London—so that they could get admission to any university in America. Nitasha and Shakuntala went to this Rutgers, not far from Hari at the time. Baby sent

Shawn and Sheela to live with her husband's sister in California. "Why are you sending them that side?" I asked. "They can live with me and Hari in New Jersey." We needed more family. In America, no one cares. Every third person is divorced; children grow up without fathers, without even roofs over their heads, worse than India, where families may be homeless, living in the streets, but at least they live together.

Life without her husband is a life that every wife fears, no matter how she may have lived with the man she married. In America, they leave the old in hospitals to die alone with only strangers to care for them. I have seen it. It is the way that Jill Gill disposed of her own mother. It is the way, God forgive my son, that my own sick husband died, machines keeping him alive after he had already left us, me, my daughters and my son, though all of my life I had heard that American medicine could cure anyone.

Sometimes while I sit in my son's new California house, waiting for him to bring his family home from what even *he* calls the *family* business, I feel as if I have been condemned to prison, where no one but the night watchman can speak my language. When I can no longer bear the hours in my cell, I take the long trip back. Delhi does not feel, at first, like the place of exile it was in 1947. I see my brothers and their families, my sisters, friends who had to leave the Punjab when we left. We have so much to do, for a time. But then I feel alone. My brothers and my sisters live surrounded by their children and grandchildren. And without children, a woman has no purpose, even when her children have had children of their own. I fly to Bombay; I can stay with Jeety now as long as I want. Her mother-in-law, old Kamla Sahni is dead, and the sons of Prakash's brothers have their own flats all over the world where their mothers and fathers have gone to live, leaving Jeety and Prakash with more rooms than they need, long after they needed them. Or I fly to Africa. Harwinder's son keeps her in Nairobi. He refuses to go for his college to America. Just like his father. Her husband cannot keep her there. He rarely even sleeps at home. His old mother and I sit all day. We have nothing to talk about; she has so rarely been to India and was not even there when the Partition cut my father's farm in two. I spend months in London too. Baby is wise to keep herself apart, with Indian ladies, who do not invite their British neighbors to their parties, just as their neighbors' ancestors saw fit to separate themselves from Indians in Delhi, Bombay, even our Punjab. It is America that has corrupted the children.

Harwinder's daughter may never be married. A girl may make a mistake. Anyone may make mistakes. But this girl wears her sin for all the world to see. Without ever marrying the boy of her choice, she had a child.

If a girl refuses to marry, she must make a lot of money—as a doctor in this country, a businesswoman or a doctor of engineering like my son. Jeety's daughter could not get admission to any medical school, and she will not consent to marry the boys her mother finds for her. I do not know what is wrong with that girl, so pretty, a good, homely girl, it is a mystery that she has not attracted boys the way that Rosa, my son's daughter, even when she was fourteen, fifteen years old, brought boys home. I blush, but it is the truth.

In America, my son has told me, all girls choose for themselves. And marriage is such a matter of choice that women marry women, men marry men, girls have children without bothering to marry. Choice may be a good thing. If I had ever had the choice, maybe my life would have been different. But America has gone too far.

"Sell your gold," I tell my daughters. "Join your children in America. They *need* you. It does not matter that they are not settled. We will settle them in California. Hari has a big house in this Half Moon Bay. The family *must* be together." America is so much bigger than I thought.

The longer I am left alone in my son's house, the more I think; and the more I think, the more I fear. In one dream I saw my husband standing at the foot of the narrow bed my son bought for me in

California. I saw my father at his right-hand side. Both said, "This time you need not pack a thing." For this exile I will leave behind the very body that my father gave my husband to bear the children we have sown all over the world. This old body, fat and sluggish, that gives me more pain than pleasure, how can I ever leave it?

If we cannot cast off the illusions of this life, the soul must return in another body, as unlike this old, frail body as East to West. "This is your last illusion," the gods say to the hero, as he goes off to eternity alone, tricked into believing he has heard the voices of his family, who have all died before him. I sit in my son's empty house missing the daughters that I sent away in the hope that they might one day bring the family together. And I pray to be delivered from this exile into which we all must go alone.

4 The Curse of Life

Shakuntala Kaur (Kunti)
New Brunswick, New Jersey

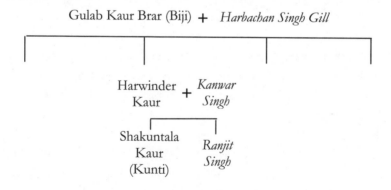

Gulab Kaur Brar (Biji) + *Harbachan Singh Gill*

Harwinder + *Kanwar*
Kaur *Singh*

Shakuntala
Kaur
(Kunti)

Ranjit
Singh

Thus does a maiden grow into a wife;
But self-willed women are the curse of life.
Kalidasa, Shakuntala, IV, ii

I KNOW WHAT my mother and father will say. Or Biji, my mother's mother—an old, bitter exile of the same British politics that moved my great grandfather from India to Africa, where even my father's father was born. My grandmother lives with my uncle just a few miles to the west. Uncle Hari talks about moving to California, starting his own business, but he still works for Ortho, still lives in New Jersey, which is why my parents sent me here instead of the University of California or Arizona or anywhere nice. Call my mother in Nairobi, Kenya, and her brother and mother will be here, to rush me to a hospital or worse. As if I didn't know myself what to do so none of them will ever know.

But every time I close my eyes, I finally remember the illustrations I blocked on three years ago, when I took my Developmental Biology final—fertilized egg at twenty-four hours, zygote at ten days.

I don't get up until I hear Asante opening the fridge.

"What you doin' home?" he asks, his dreadlocks flat on one side.

"I took the day off."

"Sick?"

"A little." I open a bottle of mango juice my uncle Hari sent home with me the last time my grandmother called and insisted I spend the weekend with them. It's the only thing I've found that cuts the nausea.

"My mom always made me soup."

"Oh, please." I pull my dressing gown around my waist, still, thank God, as thin as it has always been. Though I've slept with this man, though he's lived with me for five-six months, I do not feel comfortable standing beside him in a flimsy wrap, especially while he's moving around the kitchen in nothing but his shorts. When I first saw his tangled, twisted hair carelessly tied back in a net, as if to say, "Okay, for the tips I'll follow Health Department rules," I understood what had been bothering me about the boy I had been going out with. Asante's skin was not much darker than mine, but his hair, his chocolaty eyes set above his gleaming cheekbones won out over

Doug's blue-veined skin, his colorless eyes and lank, blond hair. I begged my cousin Nitasha to go back to the same restaurant with me the very next night and kept her drinking spritzers until Asante finished working. We dropped her home and drove until he confessed he could not take me home. He was living in his car. "You can stay with us," I said, and we made love in the living room, not quietly enough for my prudish cousin.

She moved out not two months later. "He won't stay forever," I said. "Just until he gets a place."

"He's got a place," she said. "Ask him to pay the rent."

But Asante never had any money. Like the Africans I had grown up with, he lived at a slow pace; he didn't worry about things he could not change—like the future he did not believe in or his poor, unhappy past. He only worked as much as he had to; he spent his time off working out or running by the river with his friends, who were just as laid back as he was. I found his day-to-day existence a relief compared to my parents', even Doug's constant "What-are-you-going-to-do-with-your-life?" I'd go to grad school—in chemistry or anthropology, I can't decide which—but my parents refused to send me any money. They will pay for medical school, they say, they will borrow if they have to, but if I want a master's or a PhD in such an impractical subject, I will have to pay for it myself. Asante never finished college, didn't feel the need. I can understand that. Even with a bachelor's I could not find a better job than assistant in a lab I worked in part-time before I graduated.

He's popping the tab on a can of Coke when I remind him: "Do you remember how you told me you never knew your father?"

He nods, a swig displacing the Adam's apple on his yellow throat, peppered with coarse, black stubble.

"I never understood if that was because he deserted you or your mother never told him she was pregnant."

His thick lashes droop over his glossy eyes, as if to ask me why I've brought up what he'd already told me months ago. His father was a white man, German; Asante has never seen even a picture of him. His mother was of West African extraction. I'll never meet her. Medical expenses ate up everything she had before the cancer killed her, and Asante could not get enough financial aid to both live *and* go to college, even if he wanted to. So we have a lot in common, except that my mother and father are still alive, still together, a mystery considering the fights that from time to time drove everybody but my grandmother out of our house.

"Mama only told me that he went back to Europe," Asante says. "She never heard from him again."

"Well," I say. "I'm telling you."

"Tell me what?"

Tears prevent me, and I wish someone would just come in and let him know. And I could not wait to get away from my mother precisely because she was always telling me what to do. "Open your English book, child," because I was going to America, and I was going to have to be excellent in English. Forget about the fact that I had always attended American schools, that all of my instruction was in English. English was the subject my mother had wanted to study herself, but I was not to take any courses in English literature beyond those required to prove my proficiency to these Americans. "Study your maths. Science is the most important," so that I could be a doctor. And though African history wouldn't do me any good, "Memorize everything," so that I would come first in my mother's school and she could brag to her fellow teachers, to all of the Indians in Nairobi, to the family.

Asante sets his can on the counter and steadies my shoulders with his big, firm hands. "You ain't pregnant, are you?"

I cringe. I can almost hear my father calling me every name he can think of for a girl who would sleep with a man she has not been married to, does not even *want* to marry, may not even like. But Asante's chest is so close, warm and naked that it draws me to him, and I lean against it sobbing like a child.

"Holy shit," he says, pushing me away. He disappears into the living room. I can hear him pulling on his jeans. I sit down behind the little table Nitasha bought at a yard sale and drop my face into my hands. It feels good to cry. Maybe if I cry hard enough, the baby will let go and leave me all alone. The way Asante backed away from me, The way my mother and father put me on a plane to colonize an already colonized continent so that they could send my brother to tear up the Turnpike with his motorcycle—any day now, the way they talk—then move in themselves. So they could chide me in person about not having a better job, not getting married to someone on the list of professionals and businessmen they have been compiling ever since I left Africa.

Asante comes back into the kitchen in his jeans and T-shirt. "Got to think about this." He crosses the living room and opens the door. "I ain't leaving."

When I hear the door close, I feel as betrayed as the legendary character my mother named me for. In the myth Mum told me, Shakuntala is left to bear her child alone. A man doesn't have to admit it is his baby. Even if Asante makes it back, accepts this baby, like the king, at last, I'm still in trouble. His tips have never helped pay the bills, and my parents will never accept him. He is everything they thought they were keeping me away from by sending me to those exclusive, American schools and threatening to beat me, cut me off from the family if I ever dated an African or European. Then when I thought I fell in love with an Indian, he was forbidden because he was Muslim! I feel a smile coming on. Just let them try to keep me away from that biology they wanted me to study so they could impress the neighbors. I can hide biology for only so long. My uncle is certain to find out. He might not call my mother. But my grandmother, who is living with him, will.

I telephone my cousin, and she puts me on hold every time a doctor's office calls to match a patient with a bed. I blurt out, "I've got to call Nairobi" and "I'm going to have a baby."

"Your parents found a husband for you?"

"I can hear them now! 'Never speak of this to anyone. We will never find you a husband!' Under those circumstances, who would want one?"

"'Kuntala," she says; it's what she calls me when she's feeling close. Everybody else shortens it to Kunti. Though "Kunti" is an entirely different mythological woman. "You're not trying to tell me you're pregnant, are you? You told me you were not in love with Asante. Why did you sleep with him if you're not in love with him? Is he still living with you? It *is* Asante, isn't it? Is *he* the father?"

"Of course he's the father. You don't know what a man can do, Nitasha. Once you've had sex it doesn't matter *what* you love. I didn't love Doug either. I wish I *could* love someone—the way I thought I loved Kabir," my first, the Muslim, literally the boy next door.

"What does Asante say? Did you tell him? You can't have it. Will he pay for an abortion?"

"What makes you assume I'm having an abortion?"

"How are you going to support a baby? You can't marry Asante."

"*You* can't tell me what to do." I slam the receiver down. I don't know why I talk to family. Even Nitasha never understood me. She couldn't stand it when Kabir came to stay with me, and then when I broke up with him she called me promiscuous. And I *never* even asked what she did with her girlfriend when they slept in the same bed on Lalita's visits from Canada.

I count eight hours. In East Africa the sun has just gone down, in a matter of minutes, without hanging in the sky the way it does in New Jersey. I close my eyes and remember the night birds calling in the avocado trees, frogs and crickets louder than anything I've heard in this cold country, except the traffic. Then I remember my mother hugging Kabir's mother at one of the parties we were always going to, not ten minutes after Mummy reminded me that if I so much as talked to Kabir she'd lock me in my room. And I'm glad to be in America, even if I *have* been lonely.

It's too early for a party; Mummy might just be home. Where Daddy might be is anybody's guess. I dial the number. Mummy picks up. "Shakuntala! Why are you calling? Are you sick?"

"Not entirely."

"You know how difficult it is to get money out of the country—"

"I could use some money—"

"No shopping! No going out. You must save your money for your studies. If you complete a PhD maybe those American medical schools will accept a foreign student. You must apply for immigration. Student visa will not last . . ."

The hook-up is by satellite, so only one person's voice can be heard at a time. Unless Mummy stops talking, she will never hear me. "Mum!" I shout, "Mummy!" in the hope that she might stop and listen.

"Talk to your father, child. We are having a party."

My father gets on, a rare night at home, and I wonder why they entertain when he doesn't even sleep there anymore. "Let me talk to Mummy," I say, in tears again, while Daddy tells me one more time to study, not to worry about money, and hands the phone to my grandmother, who updates me on which body parts are paining and tells me to come back and marry one of the boys she has her eyes on for me. I put the phone down, sobbing.

I'm cried out enough to be writing Mum a letter when Asante comes back. He stops in front of me, where I am sitting on the floor, his high tops so big above my knees that I feel like a bug about to be squashed. "I would *never* abandon my child," he says. He squats, his thighs jutting out on either side of me like a trap set for some fur-bearing animal, and I can smell his sweet, musky scent. "We must take responsibility. Minister Farakhan says."

So I *am* my mythic namesake, the king acknowledging the mother of his child by order of the gods. But Louis Farakhan is no god I ever gazed at on the walls of the temples my aunt Jeety dragged me to on my family's trips to India. And Asante is no king, though who knows if his ancestors were royal to the tribe before they found themselves chained in the hold of a ship to America?

He's still living with me ten days later when my mother calls. "How can you do this to your family? Have we not raised you—?"

"I haven't *done* anything to anybody but myself."

"How will I show my face? How can you ever come to us? Even *I* will never be invited—"

"I thought I was supposed to settle in America!"

"Your uncle will take you to a doctor. It will not be painful. You must move into your uncle's house."

"You can't tell me to kill my baby," I say, several times to make it through the satellite black out.

I think I hear her say I can deliver it in secret, she will call my uncle, he will contact an orphanage, when my father yells, "Where was your bastard brother when a girl of this family—" My grand-mother—his mother—sobs into the receiver, "Oh, my child. Stop him. He will kill her."

"Call the police," I shout. "Police!"

I hang up and dial the house next door. Mrs. Ali has never forgiven me for her son's nervous breakdown, in Indiana after I told him to stop driving east to see me. But she's closer than the Nairobi police, and they're worse than useless anyway. I don't give her time to hang up. "Run next door! My father! He will put her in the hospital!"

Asante's not at home, so when my uncle calls, there's no one to pick up the phone and say, "Wrong number." "I just spoke to your mother," Uncle Hari says, and I breathe because she must be all right. Enough to call him, at least. I close my eyes and see Kabir's mother running across her garden, her bright salwar kameez passing through the gap in the fence Kabir and I made after my parents would not let me go to his house—or let him into ours. My father hears her pounding on the patio doors and runs out for a drink or to his mistress' flat.

My uncle's voice brings me back to my one-bedroom in New Brunswick: "I don't think you know how difficult it is to raise a child in this country without the big house, the servants, your parents' money."

"I know what I'm doing."

"Jill and I have given you so much," he says, "but we are not willing to finance your lifestyle." So he's parted with a hundred here, a hundred there. It's *nothing* to him! And only when my mother called and begged him. He is so American! He has to think before he gives a cent to the family. "Who's the father?" he asks. "Are you getting married?"

"Whether I get married or not is not the issue."

"Kid, you'll have a baby. Some day, when you have an income."

"I don't have the choice to wait until I strike it rich."

"If it *is* a question of money—"

"You can't *buy* my baby," I say, and I hang up, too mad to talk to anybody. Because he is the only brother he thinks he is the head of the Gill clan.

But he doesn't care a bit about his sisters or us kids. After he had picked me up at the airport and left me at Nitasha's apartment, she said, "In my three years at Rutgers he has only ever called when my mother calls to tell him to. He has never dropped by, and even if he did, Jill has him too Americanized to say anything, let alone tell your mother."

When the phone rings again, I let it go, sure it is my mother's mother, the grandmother who lives with Uncle Hari. She's the last person in the family I want to talk to. She never even saw her husband before she had to sleep with him, so what can she know about love? When she had daughters instead of a son, her mother-in-law gave her boxes of coals instead of candy. So when did she ever really want a baby, no matter what it turns out to be? She thinks *she's* the head of the family. And she will take it on herself to convince me to have an abortion, hush it up, move into my uncle's house where she can keep an eye on me, and marry someone she has in mind, an Indian, Punjabi Sikh, who will keep me under lock and key so that I won't destroy the family with my taste in men.

I don't hear from anyone again, except Nitasha, for a week, long enough for my mother to realize there's nothing she can do. When I hear the ring in the middle of the night I always jump out of bed and rush through the living room to the kitchen, where the phone hangs on the wall, to pick it up before my answering machine can waste an international connection.

"Child," my mother says. She's already crying. "Who is the boy? If the family is good, you can bring him to Nairobi. We will have a wedding—"

"He hasn't got a family." I peek into the living room, where the moonlight streams through the window onto Asante shifting in his sleeping bag laid out on the floor.

"He must have *some* family, child. What is his job? Is he a student?"

"He had to drop out when his mother died. This country's not all opportunity, Mum. Especially when a man's not white." Asante sits up and peers at me through the darkness. We used to talk about this

stuff. But Asante usually works at night when he works at all, and I
have to get up in the morning.

"The boy is Indian? What is his name?"

The moonlight flecks his dreadlocks, and I think about the upris-
ings I read about in African-American history. "His name was
Stephen Chambers," I explain, "but he renamed himself. Asante.
That's right. 'Thank You' in Swahili. Christian names were given to
his ancestors to wipe out their African culture."

"He is African?"

"African-American," I say. "Black."

Asante gets up and goes into the bathroom while I listen to my
mother cry. "All this time I could not understand how you could do
that with a boy. But black? Child, they are ugly—"

"In Nairobi you *have* to tell each other Africans are ugly. Otherwise the Indians would marry them and not *be* Indians."

"You have changed. It is a curse that you and your brother are
the most beautiful children in the family. Your father is right."

"He is not right! He's sleeping with an African himself. And he
hurt you!"

"Listen, child. See reason! There's no time. Even I am controlling
my temper. Black or white if the boy will marry you, the family will
help you. We can buy a flat. Your uncle will give him a job."

"At Ortho? Uncle Hari couldn't even get *me* a job. And if you
want to buy a flat, Mum, buy one now. I don't have money for the
rent!"

"Child, you *must* marry someone. Babies may be premature, but
not *that*. You can send the baby to Nairobi—"

"You wanted to kill it!"

"That is your father's opinion. I know why you want the baby. If
he is a son, he will look after you—"

"I will not have you raising my baby the way you raised me!"

"How can you say such things?"

When I hang up, Asante comes through the dark and puts his naked arms around me. I tear my nightgown pulling it over my head. As a lover he has always been urgent, strong, but almost distant in the way he works his big, long body against mine. We're down to making love only when the tension builds to a point where I would do it with almost anybody. I don't love Asante, Nitasha is right about that, even as I swore I'd loved Kabir. Stealing moments through the hole in the fence, Kabir and I talked constantly about being together in America. But when I saw him in New Jersey I wondered why I'd longed for him so much. And that has been the only love I've ever known.

A week after Mum's last call I'm back to my routine—going to the lab, even when I feel like throwing up, falling into bed before Asante leaves for the restaurant. It's the middle of the night when I hear somebody knocking. I wake up thinking it's a dream. I shout, "Asante!" to let the knocker know a man lives in my apartment. When I hear his bare feet padding to the door, I breathe. The latch clicks. I hear a shout, the door hits the wall, and I rush out of the bedroom. Asante's in his shorts, dreadlocks flying, grappling with a man almost as tall, his head bulging unnaturally in the dark—an afro? I run across the room to pick up the phone. *911*. As I'm shouting the address, I watch Asante push the man into the hall. "Hurry, please!" The light in the hallway reveals a coil of hair untwisting as a wad of cloth pops off the intruder's head. A turban? "Daddy!"

"Whore!"

Asante grabs him from behind.

"Don't hurt him," I say, and my heart falls as my father hits the floor. A crowd of neighbors fills the hallway. "Go away," I say. No one is helping.

Asante is sitting on my father's back on the threshold when four policemen run down the hall pointing their guns. My father cries into the floorboards, kicking like a child, while two policemen, one white, one black, grab Asante's arms. He's in handcuffs by the time I find the voice to say, "He's innocent. He was trying to protect me."

My father wails.

A woman, black, stuffed into a uniform just like the men's, takes out a pad and pen and asks me, "Name?"

"Do you have to write a report?" I ask. "My father has just arrived in this country. He didn't do anything."

"Didn't do anything?" Asante asks.

"He was angry. We were scared when he came in."

"He jumped me," Asante says.

"Domestic?" asks one of the policemen still holding Asante's arms. The woman nods. She insists on taking our names.

My father sits on the floor, his cheeks, even his beard wet with tears. I kneel down beside him and smell the liquor on his breath.

"Anyone in need of medical attention?" the policewoman asks as the men unlock the handcuffs.

My father addresses the police directly, slurring only slightly: "Doctor will not be necessary. Only you must arrest this boy."

"Arrest who?" Asante shouts.

"You ain't going to call us back," one policeman asks, "if Kanwar Singh here loses his temper again?"

"You can get a restraining order, you know?" the policewoman tells me. "He can be deported." My father sobs, and I feel so much like my mother that I want to call Nairobi and apologize—for all the times I thought that he would stop if she would only do what he wanted. At the same time I want to comb my father's hair, wrap it on top of his head and tie his turban.

The police leave, sliding Daddy's suitcase inside the door. "Leave him here," Asante says, pulling me toward the door. "My car's out front."

"I can't," I tell him. "He's my father."

My father shouts, "I will not allow this boy inside my house."

"I'm no boy," Asante says.

"Daddy, you can't call a black man a boy."

"He is wild animal," my father says, peering up at Asante, who is standing, bare chested, his hands on his hips, more like some African god than even a human animal. "He is no more black than that Nitasha."

"His ancestors were kidnapped from the continent *your* grandfather was sent to," I say, "because the British didn't trust Africans to run their precious railroad."

"My grandfather built a fortune in Africa," my father says. "This boy is practically white. What has he done?"

"I ain't white," Asante says.

"His ancestors were raped by their white masters," I say.

"I'm out-a-here," Asante says, pulling his jeans over his white boxers.

"Yes, you go," my father says, and to me, "You must see a doctor."

"You leave Kunti alone," Asante says. "It's her baby. It's *ours*. If she wants it—"

"How can she know what she wants? She is just a girl."

"I'm twenty-three!"

"It is a father's duty to settle his children. How can you do this to your family?"

"In this country," I say, "you can do anything."

"Unless you're black," Asante says.

"I told your mother. There are colleges in India. Even in Nairobi. Now I have no daughter." He feels his head, looks around and picks his turban off the floor. "Where is a mirror? I must fix my turban."

While he's in the bathroom, I feel more uncomfortable with Asante than I've ever felt. All I'm wearing is the thin, torn nightgown I took off the last time we made love. I go into the bedroom for my dressing gown.

"This is crazy." Asante follows me. "Why didn't your mother call to tell you he was coming?"

"He probably left without telling her," I say. "Let me call her."

Daddy comes out of the bathroom, his turban wrapped haphazardly, and grabs his suitcase.

"Where will you go?" I ask. I try to hold him but he pushes me away and carries his bag out the door. I wonder if he has Nitasha's address, Uncle Hari's. I feel more alone than I have ever felt, and I have lived six thousand miles from my family for the past six years. I rub my belly underneath my dressing gown. "Bring my father back," I tell Asante. "He *has* to understand."

"How is *he* going to understand?" He closes the door, separating my new life in America, a life nobody in the family could ever have imagined, and my father. I could catch up with him, fall at his feet, but he will only forgive me if I sacrifice the life inside me for the life I left when he and my mother put me on the plane.

Asante walks me into the bedroom saying, "Don't you worry. He'll be all right. He *got* here, didn't he?"

He holds me in his lap and kisses me, but I cannot respond. "I will never run out on my kid," he says. "Even if he does something bad."

"Have *I* done something bad?"

"Not in *my* life." But his life is so different from the life my father gave me, keeping my mother down in Africa, where so much energy is spent separating Indians from Africans, women from men, that it's no wonder I feel trapped, even in America. Two oceans lie between the country where I live and the country my mother left to marry my father. I try to push Asante off. I must call Nitasha, call my uncle, tell them to look after Daddy, but Asante's strong, and something in me needs to cling so badly that I pull him to me, wrap my legs around him. Then I close my eyes, lying underneath him, and I give myself up to the cold, cold current of those seas, chained to a decision that I did not, cannot, will not ever make.

5 Abduction from the Seraglio

Ranjit Singh
Nairobi, Kenya

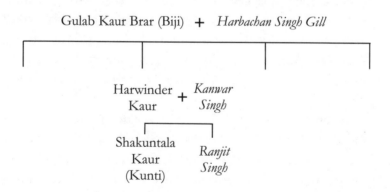

I MET HER in London. In my cousin Shawn's favorite black and tan. We're the only cousins the same age. Our mothers are sisters. We were always begging them to fly us to each other's house—him to visit me in Nairobi, me to spend school holidays with him in London.

I was staring at her long black hair, blending with her straight, black dress, like some kind of head-to-floor-length veil. "Club full of girls," Shawn said, "like a bloody harem. And you have to get obsessed with the one dancing with a big, fat, dangerous Arab!"

Even Shawn looked older than seventeen. That's why our mothers were afraid of us. We're tall, almost six feet. If we grew our beards only our eyes would show, our fair, straight noses. But I had *never* wanted to cover up my face with a beard like my father, to wrap my hair up in a turban. I was only ten when I scissored off the topknot my mother tied and covered with a swatch of cotton every day. When she saw me, strands all jagged in my face, she screamed. "You are not my son!" sort of thing. Daddy was even worse: "You think you are such a man, you can do what you want without regard for family?" I had a black eye after that. My first. I tried to ride my moped out the gate. Our guard knocked me off the bike, and my grandmother— Daddy's mother—pushed me into the car and called the driver.

Our driver recommended the barber. Sikhs, what did we know about shaves and haircuts? "This boy, he don't need a haircut," the barber said, as he evened up the ends. "He need a doctor."

My grandmother's doctor put an ice bag on my eye and said, "Ranjit Singh, you are a Sikh Sardar, like me. You should not have done such a thing. Your father is an angry man. You know that. Even we know it. We are used to Kanwar's temper."

He gave me candy and told me to go home, grow my hair, and beg my father's forgiveness.

I did not. Mummy, black and blue herself by the time my grandmother got me home, muttered, "It will all grow back." But I found scissors at school if I couldn't find a pair at home, my friends' houses, Shawn's when I was in London. Shawn's Mum, my Mum's sister, never tied Shawn's hair; even his father had not kept the turban since he had left Africa for college. But there was no escaping our ancestors. Every day at four o'clock the stubble of a full Sikh beard invaded our Punjabi faces.

So when the girl looked back, what did she see? Two men. And Shawn and I had always had to fight them off. At Nairobi parties I took them in their rooms while in the garden their fathers got drunk and their mothers stuffed their mouths. The Arab saw her looking at me and grabbed her arm. Dance steps turned to staggers. I was on him. He went down as easy as my father when he was as drunk. Shawn tried to pull me off. "Ranjit! Are you mad?"

The girl stood staring, hands covering up her sharp cheekbones. I jumped up, grabbed her wrist, pulled her toward the door. The crowd stumbled all around us.

The motorcycle I had bought that afternoon stood sparkling with drops of rain. The girl threw her leg over the seat. An ugly gash opened in her tight, black skirt. My eyes fixed on her thigh, glowing like a beacon in the streetlight. "Go!" she shouted, twisting to look back. "He will kill me!"

I straddled the bike, kicked it into action. Shawn's bike started right behind us. I could feel the girl's bare arms around my waist, her belly bag driving into the small of my back.

"I have all the necessary papers," she shouted, "money! My sister lives in Paris! Take me!"

Gladly. I'd bought the motorcycle for a trip—Shawn's last before his family was sending him to California. We had visas for every country in Europe.

I cut the motor. Shawn tore halfway down his sleeping street, almost slid his bike out from under him turning around. I laughed. "Just go in and get our packs!"

"Ranjit, the entire Muslim horde will be on us before we cross the Channel!"

"It is true," the girl said. "He will murder us. He thinks it is his right."

I lit a cigarette. "Well, Shawn, you had better hurry."

Shawn ran down the street, past a row of houses. I got to know Zarina. That was her name. Tears rolled out of her blue-black eyes. She was shaking. I took off my jacket, slipped her cold, marble arms into the sleeves. She was everything I could not find in Africa— beautiful, exotic, older than the average, giggling Nairobi Indian, and helpless. I flicked a tear off her cheek, pulled her face closer to mine. She pushed my cheek with two cool fingers. Even I could feel the stubble. "You remind me of one boy."

"What were you doing with *him*?" I asked.

"They would not allow me to marry anyone but him. He drinks. He liked to show me off at these London discos. I have been planning my escape. Take me to the train to Paris. I have money, all the papers."

I laughed. "I'll do better than the train."

Shawn came staggering back, a pack slung over each shoulder. I fixed mine into one of the bags hung on either side of the bike. I'd balance it later. "Ranjit, you are one crazy Sardar," Shawn mumbled, as he shouldered his pack and threw his leg over the seat.

I told Zarina, "Sikhs—what we call Sardars—have been protecting women from the Muslims since the Mughals invaded the Punjab."

Europe, forests cut down centuries ago, every space used up, animals replaced with humans, clogging the streets with their little cars. I hate it. Sun shone bright across those treeless fields, then on the factories, car after beeping car, even on the wide, filled streets of Paris. Zarina shouted, "Here! Turn here!" And we zigzagged through the traffic, hardly touching the brakes. Finally in front of a row of square, stone buildings she stopped me. Shawn rode halfway down the street, as usual. "Get a change of clothes," I said, laughing at my cousin. "Money. What your sister will give."

She touched my cheek again. "You are good boys. I cannot thank—"

"Fifteen minutes," I said, "or I'm coming up."

She hurried into the building, no doorman, no key. Shawn rode up. "Let's go." I lit a cigarette. "They'll call the gendarmes, Ranjit. They know the language."

I threw my cigarette into the street and ran into the building, up three steps at a time. I could hear her, shouting in a language I will never understand. And I saw her, standing at an open door on the second story. I put my arms around her. "Come. I am your family now."

Her sister, fat, older, her round face red and wet with tears, shouted at me in English: "Do you know what you have done?"

"Abduction," I said. "The oldest way to get a date."

Zarina pressed her palms against my chest. Her sister grabbed her around the waist, then pushed her into me and slammed the door. I could hear her sobbing. Zarina hurled herself against the door. I pulled her toward the stairs. Just like home. "He will kill her if he finds me here," Zarina said. She ran down the stairs, into the street, threw her leg over the seat and said, "Take me. I have no one! Go!"

We crossed into Belgium in a matter of hours, riding through the long, bright twilight of the north. Odd the way the sun takes hours to set so far from the equator, and at different times every day. By the time we got to Amsterdam, the light was artificial.

We left her ripped dress on the floor of a cheap hotel. She was shy, pushing my hands off the sleek, torn velvet. But we smoked a little marijuana, a little more.

Shawn spent guilders, Deutsche marks, Austrian shillings, and lira to get what I was getting free. I kept all three of us high. Drugs and alcohol always worked for me. We saw more of Germany than anybody should and crossed the mountains into Italy. In Rome the last of our lira went for a bottle of red in a cafe on a street full of honking, squealing cars. Cross the Mediterranean, and the continent was mine.

"I say we cut through France back to the Channel," Shawn started, not for the first time.

"No," Zarina said, the hundredth time herself. "He will find us, kill my sister—"

"No on is going to kill anyone," I said. "Biking back to England was the family plan. Our plan is to bike along the Mediterranean, then down the Red Sea—"

"Middle East is out of the question," she said.

"We can get a boat to Tunis."

"We can't motorbike through the Sahara," Shawn said. "Can I talk to you?"

"Shawn, we're practically doing it in front of you. Anything you say you can say in front of my woman."

"You can't take her to Nairobi!"

"No one in Africa will know me," Zarina said, staring into the rush of little cars and scooters in front of us.

"You see?" I said. "It's the ideal destination."

"You'll kill yourself getting there!"

I called home. I was sick, I told them, could not ride back to London. "Sell the bike," my father said, and he wired me enough to buy a one-way ticket to Nairobi. With the lira we could get for Japanese motorcycles in Italy—a loss considering what we would have got in Africa—I bought two first-class tickets to Nairobi. Shawn took the train to London.

Imagine me, Ranjit Singh, my arm around a Persian beauty in the tight, black leathers I bought her in Amsterdam, walking out of customs into a crowd of Indians and Africans. When my mother saw me she shrieked. My father shoved her aside and walked up to check out my girl. No hug, no greeting. "Did you meet this girl on the plane?"

"This is Zarina Shabazz," I said. "I met her in London."

"Honored to make your acquaintance," she said.

Dad pressed his palms together. "Is your mother-father meeting you?"

"My mother and father live in Hong Kong," she said.

"Oh, I see. Can we give you a lift to your hotel?"

"She's not staying in any hotel," I said.

"Of course not," my father said. "Why should she stay in a hotel when she has friends in Nairobi?" He grabbed my ear and pulled me past my mother. She tottered after us on the usual high heels.

"Ow!" I pushed him off of me.

"What are you doing bringing girls from Hong King?"

"She is not from Hong Kong!" I rubbed my ear. "She's from London, and she's mine."

"You are a child," my mother said, too loudly, gaining on us. Zarina stood frozen, the crowd jostling all four of us. "You cannot marry this girl."

I elbowed through the crowd and took Zarina's arm. "We'll book a room at the Intercontinental," I said, hoping I could use my father's credit. I pulled her toward the door.

"She will stay with the Alis," my father said, right behind me. "That will suit an Arab girl."

I whispered in Zarina's ear as we dodged the taxis, cars, buses. "Convenient. The Alis live next door. My sister made a hole in the fence between our compounds. Ali's son and she were doing it. Then she did it with someone else, or there would be two Muslims in the family."

"Are they related to the Alis in Lebanon?" she asked.

"They're Pakistani," I said. "They won't bother you. The son is catatonic. Tried to kill himself, the way I heard it, but he did more damage to the ceiling than his neck."

We drove up the Alis' drive, and my mother got out and waddled to the door. Mrs. Ali came out to the car, opened the door, and took Zarina in her arms, as if she was the long, lost daughter she had never had. "You are from London, isn't it?" I heard her say, as she led my girl into her house. "I have one cousin-sister . . ."

As soon as Daddy stopped the Mercedes in our drive, I got out and walked across our compound. Behind a row of shrubs I slipped through the hole in the fence. Servants' huts stood back against the Alis' garden wall. I wondered if my sister and Kabir Ali had paid the servants for the use of their beds. I stuck my head in the first open doorway. "Juma?"

"Juma!" someone shouted. I could not see anyone in that black dark.

Juma appeared in the open doorway of another hut.

"Where did they put her?" I asked.

Juma pointed to the window. "Don't tell on me, Sahib."

I gave him a shilling, walked across the dark garden to the terrace and tapped on the window. Zarina pulled the curtain back. "Open up," I said.

"These are good people." I could barely hear her through the glass.

"And I'm not? Come outside. Finish what we started on the plane."

"Shh. I will meet you. Later. When they sleep."

I propped my back against an avocado tree. The soft fruit blackened all around me. Juma was no better as a gardener than the houseboy he was in our house before my father hit him. I lit a joint. Insects I had missed in Europe filled my ears. Time faded. I had not slept since Rome.

I woke up and saw the branches of the tree, the bluest sky in the world. I thought, *they threw me out, I'm lost, I can't get home.* Then my eyes focused on the Alis' veranda. It took half a minute to recognize the marble, the white stucco of the house. I ran toward the window. All locked up. Curtains drawn. Did she come outside and miss me while I was asleep?

I was shivering. Summer in Europe, winter in East Africa. Where could she go? She had said herself that she had no one in the world. Even *I* wished I could just start over, be a kid in someone else's house. I went home and crawled into my bed. First time since London. Motorcycles, biker girls stared down from the striped green wallpaper.

I went back there after I got up. There she was, sitting on the terrace, shelling peas. Kabir was sitting right beside her, in the white, cotton pajamas he always wore—asylum clothes. He was like a statue: pale, chiseled. His neck was thin, almost white, like a girl's, with a necklace of cruel, brown scars. My sister was as inhumane as the rest of the family.

He was spouting something in Urdu. I know words of it here and there: something, something "star," something "rain," and a question I *half* understood as "who makes the eyes of women as intoxicating as the strongest wine?" As if *he* would ever know.

Zarina smiled at me and sighed. "I only understand a few words, but the poetry—"

I flicked a pea pod off her hand, grabbed it, pulled her through the Alis' compound to the fence. Kabir stared after us, an inmate serving time while we more clever prisoners escaped.

We cruised the streets, riding slalom around buses, taxis, Mercs, Land Rovers. After dark we hit the discos, drank on my father's account. I told chaps I knew from school, some I'd seen almost every week at the never-ending parties my parents had dragged me to: I was taking this girl to America; I would become a millionaire, like the Americans they read about in magazines. It would be easy for her to marry me—her brutal husband wouldn't want her anymore. And I had never lost a fight for anything I wanted—cutting my hair was supposed to kill my father, motorcycles were supposed to kill *me*.

When the clubs closed, I drove us both to my house. Our guard opened the gate. Zarina hopped off the bike and started running toward the fence.

"No," I said, catching up with her and pulling her back by her thin, long waist. "You stay in my room."

She pushed against me, then gave up, let me hold her in our garden in the dark. "For myself I do not care," she said. "You saved my life. What else do I have to thank you? But that sick boy—"

"Kabir? What do you care—"

She put her fingers to my lips. "He will worry."

The sprawling, eight-room house I had grown up in shot a rectangle of light into the dark. The garden swallowed up my girl, the black leather, her black hair. I stared after her.

"You must go to America," my mother said, blocking the light streaming from the kitchen.

My father added, right behind her, "Take your sister to the doctor."

"Kunti's sick?" I turned back, walked across the patio and shoved past them into the kitchen. A golden opportunity, now that my sister had finally given herself a disease. "Sure," I said. "Two tickets, and I'll do your dirty work."

My mother slapped me. I raised my hand. My father grabbed my wrist and wrenched my arm behind my back before I could flip him onto the floor. "If I weren't drunk," I said.

"Idiot!" my father said. "You think the girl wants you?"

"She is pregnant," my mother said, her hands rising to her face as she broke out in sobs.

"She told *you*?" I asked.

"It is your sister's dirty work," my father said. "I must go myself. How can I trust this boy to clean up after his sister in his father's good name?"

In my father's name I lifted a bottle from the dining room. I would not have minded if *my* girl were having the baby. But my sister? I laughed, took a swig, carried the bottle outside. I climbed through the hole in the fence. The Alis' garden was completely dark. I stumbled a little as I walked across the lawn, toward the light in the window of the room in which they'd put Zarina. When I got to the veranda, I tiptoed.

There she was, my girl, sitting in the middle of the bed, changed into a white Punjabi suit, as if she were one of their people. The door opened and Kabir came in. I raised my bottle like a club. He sat on a hard-backed chair, like the cold, stiff corpse he was. The window was open, the stupid fools. I could hear Zarina: "What choice did I have? That Ranjit. Say what you will. He was my fate. For so many weeks I carried papers. Once I tried to run with—"

I swung the half-full bottle over my head and flung it at the window. Zarina screamed. Glass shattered over the white carpet. Kabir covered his head and shoulders with his arms. Mrs. Ali rushed into the room, shouted, "Guard! Police!" Servants rushed out of their huts. Lights went on all around me on the terrace. The Alis' guard pushed me to the ground.

Kabir's mother shouted a string of Punjabi curses I had never heard in the mouth of a woman. "I will shift houses!" she ended. "You Singhs are the wildest animals in Africa!"

"Zarina," I shouted, out from under the bodyguard, who was sitting on top of me. "You might have gone with anyone, but fate chose me. You belong to me. This is not some whore's only gift! I saved you from your husband!"

Where she had come from she could be stoned for such information, her long, black hair shaved off, her round, full breasts, the hot fold of flesh she could not control when I was in her.

"You sex-crazed fool," she shouted. "You are no better than the man you took me from!"

Kabir spoke very slowly, so softly I could barely hear it. "Leave her alone, Ranjit. She is a Muslim woman."

"Was my sister Muslim?"

"Go back to your territory, animal!" his mother shouted.

I would have thrown myself right through the window if I could have climbed out from under the big, black hulk who sat on top of me. Two other servants helped him drag me to the compound gate and throw me into the road. I could hear our servants shouting with the Alis' servants in the dark. I could not see anything except the lights around the Alis' house, servants darting in and out of their thin beams. I ran through our gate, left open when our guard jumped up to help the Alis. "What have you done now?" my mother shouted.

"Where are you going?" I heard my father.

I could not stay. Not now. Not without her. And they say my father married for love. The whole family bragged about it: *Harwinder did not go for an arranged marriage.* And my sister?

Love does not exist. It is a trick, an illusion.

I opened up into the dark, the only light the dull, yellow glow of Nairobi disappearing fast behind me. I did not know where I would sleep that night, if I would ever sleep. But I knew some things. And I could feel them hurling me into the night.

6 Fast Friend

Shawn Singh Arora
San Fernando Valley, California

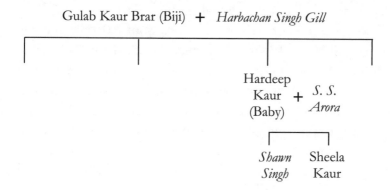

Gulab Kaur Brar (Biji) + *Harbachan Singh Gill*

Hardeep Kaur (Baby) + *S. S. Arora*

Shawn Singh Sheela Kaur

I'M SITTING ON the beach in Malibu watching my cousin Chand bob up and down on the Pacific. I tried surfing. Too much work for so little fun. My cousin Ranjit on my mother's side used to take me to Mombasa on my trips to the Kenyan branch of the family. Not much surfing in England, where I grew up.

My little sister's propped up on her elbows sulking on the sand. She's always whining. Lately it's been "I can't stand it. Why can't I move out like you and get a life?"

"You've got a life. Mum gave it to you," not admitting to wanting a girl, or even a second child, even now, fifteen years too late to *do* something about it.

"So she sends me six thousand miles away," Sheela says, "to live with a woman so paranoid she keeps me locked inside, except when her precious son breaks down and takes me to the beach."

That *woman* is our father's sister, Mona Soni. "If only she knew the boys and girls our Chand Kutta plays with," I say. We call our cousin Moon Doggie in our parents' language. I turn away from the other moon dogs lolling on the waves to catch their sun burnt, streaked-blonde bitches packing up their sunscreen, bottled water, and designer towels, wrapping sarongs around the magnificent gluteals bulging from their thongs.

My sister jogs me to attention. "Why does she insist *our* friends be Indian? *Her* son is the only Indian on the beach—except for us."

I have to force my eyes away from so much parboiled flesh. "You're too honest," I say. "You want to bring your boyfriends into the house."

"I *have* no boyfriends! I have *friends*. Mum and Daddy let us play with anybody—Arabs, Pakistanis, Africans, even Cockneys. Remember?"

"Well, in case you haven't noticed, we're not in England any more." Haven't been for almost a year. By the time Uncle Ned—that's what he calls himself; his name's Narinder—brought our Aunt Mona to California, our father was already established in the capital of the empire, sunset or not. Mona sponsored Daddy for permanent residence in the United States, but that was just to make it possible for me and Sheela to get in-state tuition, jobs, American passports eventually, coveted by everybody in our family. He may follow us when he retires, but not before. He's in management; he shakes his head at the very thought of working his way up the corporate ladder on *this* side of the Atlantic. To start his own business "sounds like too much work." He is always reminding the family of the hours he saw my Uncle Hari, my mother's brother, working at the pharmaceutical corporation where he manages a department in New Jersey. Then my father laughs and says, "Americans don't know how to live."

Mum doesn't like the lifestyle either, based on observations of Aunt Mona's daycare subsidies to pay the mortgage and my aunt Jill's series of thankless office jobs to supplement Uncle Hari's income in New Jersey. My two girl cousins Nitasha and Kunti also work at jobs they hate, also in New Jersey, and with little or no profit. "These Americans would rather go to hospital with a breakdown than admit that there is more to life than making money all day and the night. No one takes the time for family," Mum says.

I have never been able to understand the contradiction in my parents' sending me and Sheela here to finish high school. Me I can understand. I retained enough from my English school to get into Harvard, and with a degree in business, I will make a good bit more money in New York than I could ever make in England—forget about India. Mum grew up there making do with shortages and battling disease. Even she would never go back. As for my sister, she got better grades in an American school than she ever did in England. Here the standards are not nearly as high. All American high school did for me was provide me with a few good women. Maybe Mum and Daddy think they'll find my sister a richer husband here than in England, Africa or India. When Sheela's having babies in Beverly Hills, they won't have to worry about her grades. But he will have to be an Indian. Americans are poor at commitment, and their families are all messed up. I tell Sheela, "You're better off with the family. They'll look out for you. Boys can take care of themselves. I mean I *had* to move out. Even Chand Kutta sneaks out at night."

"I don't want to sleep out on the beach with moon girls," she says.

"Moon girls!"

"I just want to go to high school dances, basketball games. All I ever see are the same dull faces every week, at the same old friend and family parties. The only thing we have in common is the country our parents came from. Keep us busy with each other and we won't—we can't—make American friends. Aunt Mona won't even let me stay after school for drama practice because she's afraid I'm back stage getting pregnant. *You're* more likely to come home with a paternity suit—"

"Me? Diane's on the pill! Has been since before I hooked up with her." Nice girl. Californian. God, I love that little tan line on the belly. "They have nothing to worry about with me. I can't raise a family with a California girl. Besides, I already know who I'm going to marry. Rani. I told Dad to arrange it. Of course I won't be ready for another ten years."

"You're a hypocrite," she says. "You're as bad as Aunt Mona."

"Excuse me?"

"You wouldn't consider marrying any of those girls you use."

"How do I use girls? And how could I marry anyone but Rani? She's perfect—smart, stylish; she comes from a rich, Punjabi family; we won't have any differences with a match like that. If you feel so strongly about committing me to girls I'm not committed to, maybe it's a good thing Aunt Mona locks you in. She's not letting you run off with a California boy for a reason."

"This is not about running off with California boys. Even I would trust Mum and Daddy to find me a better husband than I could find on my own. It's got to be easier than dating."

"How would you know if you're not sneaking out with boys?"

"Who are you to call me a liar? Fucking anyone you please—"
"Watch your language! I'll tell Aunt Mona—"
"Go ahead and tell her, asshole. Maybe she'll kick me out."
"Where did you learn such language!"

Chand drives us back through the canyon, his van smelling of dead sea animals and my sister's sunscreen. I tell her, in my perfect, Chandian-American English, "Forget about it. Do your homework. I'll call you," and I get out at the Roses' three-bedroom ranch. Scott's room, in the back, overlooking a small, walled-in patio of pink concrete, has bunk beds, and I took the top, which had not been used for sleepovers since grade school. In the fall Scott's room will be empty, like his sister's. Still, I can't see my sister moving in. I'm hardly ever there. I'd have my own car if my father would send me the money. Sheela isn't even old enough to have her license.

I walk in and I can tell immediately something's wrong. Sandy, Scott's mother comes out of the kitchen and asks if we can talk. Her little mouth is tight, her hair stiff, like straw, standing out at her blue-veined temples, where she's run her fingers through it, what she does when a case has her stressed. For a moment I think she must have been talking to Diane's parents, must have found out we've been doing it in the Toyota Diane got as a graduation present. Or maybe Diane's parents just suspect and called and asked Scott's family, in the absence of my father, to have a little talk with me—about what I wasn't sure: birth control, AIDS, monogamy. God forbid she might be pregnant. Sheela couldn't be right. I'm suddenly afraid that Diane's parents might have driven over after work and are in the kitchen waiting for me. "Sure," I say, trying to maintain the cool I've been cultivating since shifting to California. "About what?"

I breathe again when I see only Dave, Scott's father, sitting at the butcher block. He leans over the table and, as he does every time he sees me, shakes my hand. Then he runs his hand over his bald spot while Sandy tells me, "It's Scotty."

I almost laugh with relief. Sandy Rose sits down between Dave and me, facing the ugliest wallpaper I have ever seen—gold and brown, geometric. Then my relief turns into fear and I say, "Wait a minute. What's wrong with Scott?"

"It seems he doesn't want to go to college," Sandy says.

"What?" Fear turns into disbelief, and I say, "Scott and I took that road trip. Remember? To check out UC campuses. I mean, Santa Cruz was right up there with Santa Barbara." I keep to myself the party we crashed, perfect for Scott—tie dye, incense, Hendrix. We both got laid that night. Santa Cruz was a resounding success.

"We thought maybe Scotty might have talked to you about his plans," Sandy says, "I mean, since you're Indian."

I ignore the non sequitur—she's upset—and answer, "I told him to go to Santa Cruz. It's not Harvard, but—"

Dave says, "He wants to go to India. Stay indefinitely. In an ashram."

"Is he crazy?"

Scott is what I'd call the deep, sensitive type. We'd had conversations, sure, Scott asking me to render what little I know about Hinduism. Once, I told him, I was slapped by a friend's mother for making monkey faces at a picture of the god, Hanuman, thoroughly out of place hanging on her drawing room wall in London. My family is Sikh. We do not believe in Hindu gods; we don't meditate. I knew Scott was meditating, reading translations of the Sanskrit scriptures while I slept above the high intensity lamp he'd hung from the bottom of my bunk. But to give up college in this country to bum around India like some hippie was just too, too retro, as Scott himself would say. I might have been Indian, but *that* place—backward, dirty, old—had never been my home. It never *would* be. And I'd *told* Scott.

Repeatedly. Which is why, I guess, at some point, he stopped confiding in me.

"Talk to him," Sandy says.

"We've got to convince him not to give up college," Dave says. "If he wants to spend his junior year abroad—"

Sandy says, "Sheila's coming down from Berkeley."

I have never met Scott's sister, though I love her picture—blond hair the same shade though much thicker than Scott's, the same facial structure, right down to the perfect nose—which, Scott told me, had been fixed, so I wonder if his older sister's nose had been the model; or maybe they had the same surgeon. But I can't fantasize about my friend's sister. She and *my* sister share the same name.

Scott comes home from work—a concession stand on the Santa Monica pier—and I ask him what all this shit's about: his parents are upset, Santa Cruz is no Harvard, but at least it's college, and what does he expect to do in India?

"Achieve enlightenment," he says. He sits cross-legged on the plaid rug on his bedroom floor, ready to *om* himself out of the conversation.

"You're more likely to achieve hepatitis," I tell him, hopping down from my bunk.

"You don't understand. You can't. You mocked Lord Hanuman. You've never felt the peace that comes of meditation."

"No, but I've felt the peace that comes of being able to afford what I want when I want it. Without a degree, even from Santa Cruz, you'll be flipping burgers on the pier forever. How are you going to pay for a trip to India? How will you live there? Have you thought of that?"

"A plane ticket costs less than tuition and housing, and at an ashram you can live for free."

"In college," I tell him, "you can study oriental philosophy, Hinduism, Buddhism, whatever you want. India has no monopoly on that shit. Everything's on the Internet anyway."

"I've done those things—read all the books I could find, talked to the Krishnas—"

"You've talked to the Hare Krishnas?"

"I can't waste my time at Santa Cruz. If Mom and Dad won't give me the money—"

"You want your Mom and Dad to subsidize—"

"—I'll work until I have enough."

"You're obsessed! Sir Walter Scott! California hippie! At least live in my grandmother's house. I'll give you the address. In Delhi. And in Bombay my aunt Jeety's. She knows all the Hindu shrines. She'll love you."

I concede that when a man makes up his mind, you've got to let him do it. My cousin Ranjit taught me that: if Ranjit wanted to pick up an Islamic adulteress and drag her home to his parents in Nairobi, there was nothing I could do, though I could have told him he would not be able to keep her; he breaks all his toys.

I don't know if Scott's obsession is any better than a blinding love for a woman, and I admit that to his parents. But there's not much I can do to change his mind. I promise to tell my mother to alert the family in India, a friend is coming, please look after him, though what Indians can do for a spoiled California boy, I don't know.

"Well," Dave says, "if he's got to go—"

"The least we can do," Sandy says, "is see to it that he makes a stopover in Israel. I'm willing to pay for it if he stays on a kibbutz for at least as long as he stays in an ashram."

"Why a kibbutz?"

"A kibbutz is a commune too," Dave says.

"Where Scotty can get a dose of Judaism," Sandy explains. "We're so secular."

"The last time we went to a synagogue was for Scott's Bar Mitzvah. He only wanted one to get the presents, he said that at the time."

"I should have known we were neglecting his religious education," Sandy says. "Do you know what he calls Passover in this house? 'Seder in a can.'"

"Judaism is a rich religion," Dave says, "with a mystical tradition of its own. If we had only encouraged Scott to satisfy his thirst for spirituality with our own beliefs, he might not be abandoning them now."

"He doesn't have to abandon his beliefs," I say. "Just because he's interested in Hinduism. He can still believe in Judaism."

"Our religion prohibits idol worship," Sandy says. "And we have holy days."

"He can still observe them. In our family we celebrate Hindu holidays. Even Christmas."

"Well," Dave says, "everybody celebrates Christmas."

"I should never have let the kids talk me into a Hanukkah bush," Sandy says.

"But why not?" I ask. "One faith doesn't cancel out another. That's like not allowing Indian kids to play with American kids because you're afraid they'll be corrupted."

Sandy says, "Scott *has* been corrupted. Not by you, Shawn. We know you don't believe in that stuff. Do you?"

"No. That's not the point."

I tell Sheela she'll be better staying with Aunt Mona. At least our aunt and uncle are honest about separating us from the locals. The Roses invite Christians into their house, Sikhs even, to live with them, like me. But when their kid expresses a curiosity about Hinduism—okay, goes, maybe, a little bit beyond mere curiosity—they assume that to satisfy that curiosity, he has to repudiate the scriptures he memorized in Hebrew school and grow a foreskin. What is it with them? Thousands of years of being killed for being different? Sikhs have *that* in common, hundreds of years anyway. Maybe that's why Aunt Mona wants to keep us Indian. But I think we can infiltrate, enrich this country. So what if we cut our hair, forget Punjabi and live among the Christians and Jews? We still believe in one God, that God truth, and there are many paths to that God, many names, even if we don't believe a word of it.

I get up late Saturday morning, after Scott has gone to work, and when I look out the window to see what the weather is like, I have to grab the sill for balance. A sleek, bronze goddess in a black bikini lies sunning herself in a lounge chair on the pink patio. Sheila Rose's picture doesn't do her justice. And it doesn't show the breasts, barely covered, bronzed, round, as if they are not breasts at all but some perfect, as yet undiscovered fruit. Older woman. I think of Ranjit as I crank open the window. "Shawn Arora," I shout, "Scott's roommate." And I curse myself for not waiting until I could go outside and shake her hand, throw my arms around her, give her the Beverly Hills peck on the cheek. We're practically family!

She pauses midway between reclining and sitting up and peers at the house. I pray that she can see me through the window: bare chest, permanent, perfect tan, dark brown hair, cut short enough to look as good tousled as gelled—the best looking guy in the family, since Ranjit has discovered stronger drugs.

"What have you done to my brother?" she asks, a wry smile distributing the puff in her lips.

I throw up my hands. "Just the opposite," I say. "I don't believe in anything. I'm not even Hindu. Have you heard of Sikh separatism? I wouldn't go to India for my own grandmother's funeral, God forbid, and I'm going to Harvard in the fall."

"Harvard, huh?"

"Nothing but the best. Along those lines, what are you doing tonight?"

"Close the window," she says. "You're wasting air conditioning."

I jump into a pair of swim trunks and join her between the relentless walls of this southern California neighborhood. We spend the whole day talking. What a girl! She knows more about the Sikhs than I do, English politics, the current prime ministers. I impress her with the names of the sons of Kenyan politicians, just names to me, but my father went to school with them in Nairobi. She already knows she wants to go to law school. "I bet you graduate a Supreme Court Justice," I say.

She smirks.

"No, you're just so smart." And ambitious. Not anything like Diane. Not even Rani, to be truthful, who will probably study something light like literature or home economics at a small, girl's college in India and devote herself to keeping a spotless home, cooking fresh every day and raising geniuses before she takes over the books of her husband's multi-million dollar business.

I take Sheila out to lunch, where she turns the conversation to Scott, though I'd rather hear about her volunteer work with the Berkeley city council. I don't believe in sixties politics, but I believe the lifestyle was a true revolution. I'm trying to tell her about the motorcycle trip I took through Europe, the summer before I moved to California, and she says, "Scott's always been a disaffiliate. So was I. But I came back."

"Where did you go?" I lean over the little daisy on the table, not only to catch every word but to be closer to her golden skin, still glowing from the sun.

"Listen, Shawn," she says, "I'll admit. I used to date non-Jewish guys. But one day I'd like to get married; and I'd like to marry someone I love. What sense does it make to go out with someone I know I can't love?"

"You can't love a non-Jewish guy?"

"I can't *let* myself love a non-Jewish guy."

"I hear it's a simple operation," I say, throwing up my hands.

A look of confusion comes over her face. Then she laughs. "Well, I'll have to admit," she says. "That's the best offer I've ever had!"

This family is too odd, but I can't let Sheila Rose go, even for an afternoon nap before Scott comes in from the pier. "Let's lie out in the sun again," I say, moving close to her in the hall between her room and Scott's. "Or better yet in your room. Mine? Okay, Scott's."

"Don't you ever quit?"

"I'm driven. Sikhs are the Jews of India. Haven't you heard?" I put my arms around her. She presses her palms against my chest, her long nails, a light pink, just a few inches from my cheeks, and for a brief moment—too brief—she does not push away.

"I'll see you at dinner," she promises, "if you're not going out."

"How can I go out with anyone but you?"

"I told you. Don't disappoint yourself."

She closes the door on me, not fast enough to convince me that she wasn't considering.

Scott comes late that night, his scalp naked but for a tuft of wavy blond on the back of his egg-shaped head, white as a sheet, in spite of his California tan. Sandy bursts into tears. "Your beautiful blond hair!"

"You look ridiculous," I say.

"No Rose has ever insulted the family," Dave starts.

But it's Sheila who really saves the family. "Scotty, Scotty, Scotty." She gently puts her arms around her shorn brother. Go out with her? I'd marry her, if I were ready. I stay in the family room, outstaying my welcome, as Americans say, while Scott desecularizes my argument. He explains that all of the great prophets are reincarnations of the same God—Moses, Krishna, Christ. And Sheila says, "It's all right to study these things—Hinduism, mysticism. Face it. There must be as many Jewish philosophers as Jewish lawyers. But a Jew can never be anything but a Jew."

I'm looking forward to the trip back east—abandoning the Roses for the relative sanity of my Uncle Hari's mixed marriage before I move to Cambridge. The other Cambridge! Let Scott's family try to convert him back from one avatar to another. But Sheila looks so beautiful as she sits on the couch beside her brother, her hand over his hands, their faces glowing, both of them, with their own peculiar intelligence. I can't help but imagine myself standing next to her, still sore from the loss of foreskin I have always thought of as distinguishing my Muslim friends in England from Hindus and Sikhs like me. My hair will not be covered with the turban my grandfather wore but flattened with a yarmulke. I raise my foot to break a glass, beneath a canopy several shades lighter than the red and gold that will hang over the holy book around which I will lead Rani when it is time to stop being the boy I am, to become a man and take a wife.

7   *Valley Girl*

Sheela Kaur Arora
San Fernando Valley, California

Gulab Kaur Brar (Biji)   **+**   *Harbachan Singh Gill*

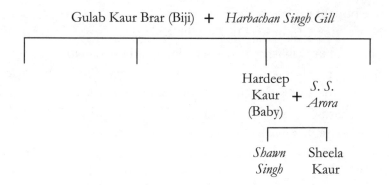

Hardeep Kaur (Baby)   **+**   *S. S. Arora*

Shawn Singh   Sheela Kaur

W HEN I GOT into Smith College, I was so happy I cried. I pressed the letter to my chest, then reread it, standing just inside my aunt Mona's San Fernando Valley house, right beside the little table where she always put the mail. The babies she took in for day care—which she sometimes left me watching while she went out shopping—crawled shrieking around me. God, it would feel good to study three thousand miles away! Aunt Mona came shuffling toward me in her fuzzy pink slippers asking, "What is it, child?" in the usual Punjabi she used with family and friends.

I answered her in the only language I could speak, besides a little Spanish—the English I had grown up with in London. "I got into Smith!" Then I had to bear her smirk of satisfaction as she smoothed her bright, blue kameez over her baggy salwars, the latest in Punjabi suits she bought on her last trip to Africa.

"Now your Mummy, Daddy will believe I made a student of you," she said in English, because she knew I'd understand.

"American schools are easy compared to the prison Mum and Daddy sent me to in England," I said, and then because I knew it wasn't California public schools that got me into Smith, "Besides, *I'm* the one who made a student out of me."

"You have no gratitude for family," she said. "I have always said."

"I have gratitude," I said. "I just like credit where credit's due."

"That is exactly what I mean."

I bit my tongue that I had contradicted her *before* I'd asked if I could call my parents. She was still considering her answer when I added, "I'll have to tell them how much to send."

"Yes," she said, "but do not talk too long."

Since it was already midnight in London, I called right away. The answering machine picked up. "Mum," I said, "it's very important. Call me no matter what time."

It was three in the morning London time. I jumped for the phone, during dinner, my aunt and uncle silent, as usual, over the usual chicken, lentils and yogurt at the kitchen table, my cousin, as usual, not home. "Nothing's wrong," I told my mother, "I just wanted to tell you. I'm so excited. I got into college—Smith!"

"Oh, that's nice. Isn't it?"

"Tell Daddy. I can't wait. As soon as graduation, I'll move to the East Coast and stay with Shawn."

My brother had been at Harvard for almost two years, and he loved it. "You cannot stay with your brother," my mother said. "His flat is small. He has roommates."

"But he's my brother," I said. "If I can't live with him, where can I live? With Uncle Hari?" My mother's workaholic brother, his American wife, and my cousin Rosa, younger than me by three years, were still living in New Jersey at the time, only a four-five hour drive from Massachusetts. Anything was better than my aunt, who had stood up from the table to lurk behind me while I added, "There's a deposit."

"Deposit?" my mother asked. "What is that?"

"Part of the tuition. You don't have to pay the full until—"

"Child, you know how expensive Shawn's college—"

"Mum! Smith is one of the top colleges in the states! Do you remember what a horrible student I was? I've done so well here that I've been accepted at a school as good as Shawn's. Almost as good."

"Colleges in California are good—"

"I don't want to stay in California. Haven't you read my letters? I'll graduate from high school in two months, and—"

"—you are resident. At a state school, like your cousin Chand, you can pay this *in-state* tuition."

"I need citizenship to get in-state tuition," I said. "I don't know if I want to be a US citizen. Besides, I've only been here for two years."

"You have been on the telephone so long," my aunt said, holding out her hand for the receiver.

"It's all right," I reminded her. "*They* made the call." I asked my mother, "Can I talk to Daddy?"

My father had always been the more rational parent, tolerant and easy going, the one who argued with my mother when she would not let us go out with our friends, the one that Shawn and I had always talked to when Mum lost control. I could not believe my ears when he said, "You will have to consider some alternative. At least for the next two years. Very good. Sheela, we are proud."

"Daddy, I can't!" I shouted. "I'm as smart as Shawn. This proves it. I want to be a doctor. I can do it."

"Doctor would be good," he said, "but your cousins—Nitasha was listed in the Bombay newspaper as first in her examinations, and Kunti graduated first in Nairobi—and neither one of them got into this medical school. Better try for medical technology or pharmaceuticals."

"You don't believe me!" I said. "I don't want to work in a pharmacy!"

Uncle Ned got up and lumbered outside to the patio, leaving his plate on the table.

"When you are married," my father started.

"Married? I'm only seventeen! Is that it? You want to get me married so you don't have to support me—"

"Do not be ridiculous—"

"—the way you dumped me on Aunt Mona?"

"You are talking nonsense," my aunt said, grabbing the receiver and fixing it to her ear. I was crying too hard to talk anyway. I would have run into the little room I had to vacate every time somebody visited from India, England, Africa or even Canada, but I couldn't bear the thought of Aunt Mona taking my father's side against me.

To my surprise she spoke to him in English: "The girl is difficult. I *told* her not to waste the money applying to colleges the family could not afford. But she would not listen. This girl *never* listens."

"That's not true!"

She ignored me. "Yes, there is a local college. But the girl does not have a car. Do you know how much it costs to keep four cars? And she is not responsible. She will go with boys. I will tell you, I have had to lock her in a room—"

"I have American friends!" I shouted. "Why is that so diffi—"

"You can *hear* the disrespect. And if I may tell you. You are my brother, but I must. I cannot take responsibility . . . You must care for her yourself . . . I will send her back."

Back? I had lived in California for two years, leading a perfectly conservative life, not even trying drugs, not drinking, not making out. Unlike her only son, who had dropped out of Cal State Northridge in his first semester—a good surf couldn't be denied for the sake of the classes my aunt and uncle had truly wasted their money on. "Give me the phone," I said, choking back tears.

"Your wife's family may take responsibility," she was continuing. "Let the girl finish her high school, what they call it, in New Jersey. See how well she studies without my supervision."

Fresh tears heated up my eyes. Nobody wanted me. I wondered how unsafe it was to sleep on the beach. Chand had often spent his nights there, partying with surfers. Where would I go, I wondered, if I could not get through the canyon—a friend's house, a homeless shelter? My thoughts were interrupted by my aunt's shout: "You dare to offer rent to your own sister? Am I a stranger that you think I will accept. . ."

She hesitated, and I grabbed the receiver and choked out, "Why did you send me?"

"Try to understand," he interrupted. "We have always been broad minded. But my sister—"

"You never tried to pick my friends. Even when Mummy—"

"She is afraid. She does not *have* a daughter—"

"You let Shawn move out when Aunt Mona found out he was sneaking out the window—"

"Shawn's a boy. He—"

"I can't *live* here!"

I threw the receiver and ran out the door, across the patch of grass in front of the six-room bungalow I had hated the moment I had seen it. Automatically I rushed toward the school bus stop, at the same pace I had taken every morning of my illustrious high school career, across streets, crying so hard I couldn't see where I was walking. No one passed me. It was too dark for joggers. Every now and then a car sped by, its headlights making the noncommittal facades of bungalows and ranches glow for an eerie moment. Once a low-rider shouted from his Olds, "Girl! Lost your boyfriend?"

I'd studied Spanish in these last two years, so I could understand when the Mexicans addressed me as if my black hair and brown skin had a history on this continent. But I could never bring home dark-skinned classmates who did not know at least the names of foods in Punjabi or Hindi. Even light-skinned classmates. I'd learned that from my aunt. I was sorry that none of the friends I'd made in spite of her lived in what I had ever thought of as walking distance. As I turned onto Victory, I wondered where to go, pounding one foot in front of the other on the unused sidewalks, on and on, past store fronts, gas stations, office buildings, restaurants, not so much to reach a destination as to put as many steps as I could between myself and my aunt. How could she accuse me of not caring about family? I had always cared. I was the one, unlike Shawn, who loved India. Mum sometimes took me to New Delhi to visit my grandmother when she was there. Or to Bombay, to my cousin Nitasha, though she is much older than me. 'Tasha was working in New Jersey at the time; I could stay with her. I'd often thought I should have gone to school in India, a boarding school, if my parents were so anxious to get me out of England. But Mum had always been snobbish about the country she'd grown up in—"India is dirty. There is no opportunity. You are lucky I was married to a man in London." Not that she believed that England had much future either: "Whole country is finished. Everyone is on the dole."

There's dirt in the New World too, though it's mostly invisible—carcinogenic. And visiting my uncle in an exclusive New Jersey suburb, she could not have seen the Angelinos on welfare. Even I had been genuinely optimistic when my mother and father told me and Shawn we would be living with one of my father's sisters, whom I had liked when she had visited us in London. And in Los Angeles, where all of the movies we adored were made!

I'd almost reached DeSoto when I turned and noticed a black Volvo following me slowly, like the low rider who had just passed. But this was no laughing Mexican-American boy. It was a man, his thin, blond hair streaked with gray. Cars screeched to a halt behind him, horns blaring, engines revving as Mercedes, Toyotas, BMW's accelerated past. He leaned across the passenger seat and beckoned through the window, a foolish smile on his pasty face. "The San Diego is straight ahead," I told him. "That will take you to the Ventura or Santa Monica." He shook his head. "Do you want the Simi? Golden State?"

"I want you." A chill ran through me. I straightened up, hurried away from the car and kept walking, as if I'd never stopped to give directions he didn't want. I could still hear the car, the horns honking behind him. This is what happens, I thought, to girls whose families abandon them. I could not help but imagine myself at the bottom of Topanga Canyon, my dark skin that no man has ever seen, except in a one-piece bathing suit, discovered by a boy hiking, scrutinized by the police, radios carrying up to the houses on the hills, the girl that Mona Soni reported missing. I could hardly breathe, imagining the man's thumbs against my windpipe.

Without turning around I walked into a Chinese restaurant, its red doors opened by a doorman in *Last-Emperor*-era silks, an artificial smile on his face. The maitre d', in a tuxedo, greeted me at the reservation desk, his smile identical to my ignorant eyes. It faded as I tried to find my breath. What would I do, I wondered, if the man came in behind me? "May I use your telephone?"

"No telephone," he said, pointing to the door behind me. "Gas station on corner."

"Someone is following me," I said, new tears spilling out of my already sticky eyes. "Please!"

He picked up a telephone receiver. "Number?"

The first number that came to mind was home—Aunt Mona's, that is. I could not call there. Run away only to ask my uncle to come and pick me up? I looked at the door. Nothing, not even customers. I was so upset that I could not remember any of my friends' numbers. Just my brother's, the one I used to call two years ago, after he had moved in with a friend, Scott and Scott's parents, David and Sandy Rose, Americans, of European descent. I recited the number. The maitre d' dialed and gave me the receiver.

"Hello?"

"Who's this?"

"Scott," he said.

"I thought you were in India. Or Israel."

"I came back. Who's this?"

"Sheela. Shawn's sister. Can you pick me up? Someone tried to kidnap me. I-I can't go home."

"Where are you?"

"In a Chinese restaurant on Victory. I'm all alone."

"Chan's Forbidden City?"

When Scott walked through the doors, as tall and awkwardly slim as I'd remembered him, thin pale hair, his face pinkened by the sun, I was sitting at a table behind a coke and a plate of dumplings I had not ordered. I stood and hugged him, I was so glad to see a friend.

"Sorry I lost touch," he said. "I was a little . . ."

"I've run away," I said. "Just like Shawn."

The maitre d' held a neatly packed paper bag in front of me. "I didn't bring any money," I said.

Scott dug into the pocket of his jeans. "No problem."

"No problem," the maitre d' repeated, refusing Scott's dollars and shoving the paper bag into my hands.

"Why are strangers so nice?" I asked Scott as we walked to his Jeep. I told him how I had been followed, how I had imagined being kidnapped, killed. "My aunt would be hysterical. I wonder if my mother and father would come for my funeral. Shawn would have to light the fire."

"Which in this country is probably a switch or something," Scott observed. "When I first came back I thought chemical weapons had hit LA I mean, where are all the pedestrians?"

"The smells are different," I said, remembering the wood fires in New Delhi. "Why did you go?" I could vaguely remember Shawn ranting and raving about Scott's choice to live in an ashram in India instead of going to college.

"I don't know," Scott said. "After I got used to the calls to prayers, the temple bells, the hymns blasting out into the streets—"

"The constant images of religion in India." I missed them too, though I hadn't grown up with anything of the sort.

"Krishna, Ganesh, Lakshmi and people's gurus all over their homes, businesses, even cars! I realized it's just the different look. Even L.A. has churches and synagogues."

"The Mormon temple!" I said.

"Most of them are not all that distinguishable from houses," he said, "or schools. American assimilation. But after I got used to minarets, turrets and domes, I began to see that just like here, it's not God that dominates everything; it's the struggle to feed yourself—or to buy nice clothes, gold, big weddings to impress the neighbors."

I sighed. He was describing my parents' world exactly, which they had exported and preserved quite well in England. My aunt Mona was trying to preserve that world in California. There were aspects of that world I liked, the clothes and gold, for instance, the turrets and domes. But live in their world and I'd have to live with my fascist aunt for another two years, so that my brother could enjoy himself at Harvard. "Can I stay with you? Like Shawn?" I asked. "At least till the end of June. Dad is willing to pay. And I want to graduate. Otherwise I'm homeless. Aunt Mona won't take me back. And I wouldn't go if she did."

Scott shrugged. "I guess you could have my sister's room. She never comes home. She's going right on for law school in Berkeley."

"Will your parents mind?"

"Are you kidding? They came to India while I was there, did you know that? Stayed at your grandmother's house. They're talking, next vacation, Kenya."

"My aunt Harwinder will treat them like kings," I promised, if my aunt didn't pack up and force Ranjit, my alcoholic cousin, to come here to live with his sister Kunti or my uncle Hari. I felt a pang of homesickness, remembering my family's famous hospitality, my aunt's palatial house and grounds in Nairobi, lush with mango trees, my grandmother's little house in Delhi, my aunt's joint family in Bombay, and South London, its Indian restaurants, Bhangra music, black and tan clubs, life.

It upset my aunt, how I could be friendly with a boy, and two years older, out of high school, which suggests experience she could not apply to her own son, though Chand hung out with a more suspicious crowd than even California Hare Krishnas. But nothing was going on between me and Scott, even in theory. He was like a brother, more sympathetic than Shawn, more sensitive.

Nothing much had ever developed between me and any boy. I liked boys; that was not a problem. But I won't have sex until I'm married. Nothing else makes sense when venereal diseases can't be cured. And I'm not ready to get pregnant, like my cousin Kunti. Besides, I'm too young to let crushes distract me from getting into the best college I can, doing well there and going to medical school to become the first doctor this family has ever seen.

When Scott and I went to pack my bags, Aunt Mona did not even say that she was sorry, did not wish me luck or even warn me. She simply hid among her day-care babies and glared.

Dad called and asked to talk to Mr. Rose. "It's perfectly all right," I could hear David respond. "We'll get her through graduation . . . Twenty five a week seems fair . . . Thanks. We've been talking about taking another vacation. It would be great to have a place to stay in London. Thanks. And a chance to meet you . . . You've got fabulous kids, real achievers. We can't do enough. They've been great friends to Scott. Good influences."

Dad told me, "Okay, you stay there till school is finished. Then you go to Uncle Hari's."

"What am I supposed to do at Uncle Hari's?"

"We will talk. If there is a community college—"

"No one said 'community college' when Shawn said, 'Harvard.'"

"Child, your mother has set her heart on settling your brother in America. And it is true he can make millions there. Let him get a job, and you will have a big house in America. We will find you a boy—"

"I don't *want* a boy. Not now, anyway. Why don't you believe that *I* might make a million in this country?" Not that I knew anyone who'd actually made a million, Harvard degree or not. At the moment I hated my brother more than I had ever hated him when he let Mum blame me for his spills and naughtiness.

Shawn called and suggested that I work for a year or two. "California or New Jersey, doesn't matter. You can save enough for tuition. UCLA, Rutgers. They're good schools. U. Mass is clear across the state. After I'm out of school, Mum and Dad will help you. Or maybe Uncle Hari. He's loaded. I'll be paying off loans."

I was not inclined to make myself dependent on Uncle Hari. And flying back to London would not solve any of my problems: what was I to do? I got off the school bus as close as I could to Chan's Forbidden City, the restaurant I'd ducked into on the night I'd run away. I'd worn one of those tight, silk Chinese dresses, which my mother had bought me on a shopping trip to Singapore. And though the boys at school had stared at me, and I had to rush from the bus to the restaurant, my backpack slung across my back, sure that I'd meet up with the black Volvo again, it had been worth looking sexier than I am. The maitre d' was so impressed, so glad to see me smiling that he showed me how to greet customers and seat them, take reservations and help the waiters with the checks—though Chinese has proven a lot more difficult than Spanish.

The Roses gave me their daughter's room. Sheila's going to be a hot-shot lawyer, she will not be coming home. But I can see a time when I'll be able to afford my own apartment. "You save that money," David says. "College is your first priority."

"I wish my parents felt that way."

"Your parents *do* feel that way. Look at your brother: Ivy League all the way!"

"Yes," I say, "but it's your daughter who's going to law school in Berkeley."

"Doesn't matter," he says. "Daughter, son. If only Scott here hadn't been distracted—"

"I'm in college now," Scott says.

"Yes, and see that you stay in."

"Girls are not assets in an Indian family." I try to understand myself. "They become a part of their *husband's* family. At least, that's what's *supposed* to happen. My family is all over the world. I never knew they were so conservative—more conservative than my cousin from Bombay."

Scott's mother, Sandy plops onto the couch beside me and says, "My whole family panicked when I brought home an acceptance to law school instead of an engagement ring. Under no circumstances would they let me move to UCLA without a husband. I *had* to marry David."

"So that's why you married me." David scowled. "And I thought it was my blond hair."

Every week or so my parents call and offer me the usual option: I can stay with Uncle Hari, though Uncle Hari has not even called to offer me a bed in his daughter's room, worse yet, my grandmother's room, where I will hear it coming and going—"We will find a boy for you. You must study [with no decent place *to* study]. Why do you need friends when you have family?" Mum and Daddy don't want me staying with Shawn because he has American roommates whom they have never met, and they are afraid I might distract him from his studies—the way we used to fight in England when I was fourteen. Shawn says nothing about moving in. Living with my cousins in New Jersey doesn't seem an option. Nitasha's apartment is only one room, and Kunti is living with the guy who fathered her baby. If I can't find anyone to live with, my parents say, I should work only long enough to save enough to buy a ticket back to London. I can live at home and save enough to go to a university there.

But is London any better than Los Angeles? I'm thinking hard about sleeping in my own room again, in the very heart of the empire that has seduced my parents' whole family without really winning their hearts. In the house where I grew up I could show them I am not the dumb, little tomboy they sent to America. I'm graduating National Honor Society, a hostess in a Chinese dress.

Without them, though, I am not merely a daughter, not the second, unwanted child; I am something that my family might never let me be. Maybe I will go someplace different entirely—China, Japan. Even India! In this family New Delhi may be the most radical point of exile on the planet!

"Sheela, you're a real individual," David Rose says, seeing me for the first time in my Chinese dress behind the reservation desk in Chan's Forbidden City.

I don't know if I'm an individual yet, if I will ever be. But I smile as I pull my Chinese silk over my thighs and show him and Sandy to the best table in the house.

8 Three Sisters

Jeety, Harwinder, and Baby
Mumbai, India; Nairobi, Kenya; London, England

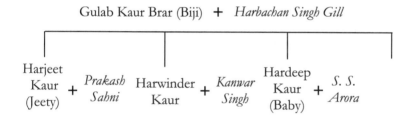

Gulab Kaur Brar (Biji) + *Harbachan Singh Gill*

Harjeet Kaur (Jeety) + *Prakash Sahni*   Harwinder Kaur + *Kanwar Singh*   Hardeep Kaur (Baby) + *S. S. Arora*

Maybe, if we wait a little longer,
we shall find out why we live, why
we suffer . . . Oh, if we only
knew, if only we knew!
          — *Anton Chekhov*, Three Sisters, *IV*

NO ONE CAN come between the sisters. We may say what we like. Let Jeety say that Harwinder, for all of her intelligence, knows nothing, and she will not listen. Harwinder can call Baby lazy or only concerned about herself. Baby may complain that as the third girl in the family she was never loved so much as Jeety, the first of Harbachan Singh Gill's children. But in matters of the most importance, *we three speak with one voice.* If only one person—our brother, his American wife, even our own husbands—says that this one is too selfish, that one stupid, the sisters will become as one: *How can you say Harwinder is too sensitive? We are all more sensitive than you! You are cold. You have done nothing for the sisters.*

And we are in such circumstances that our brother *must* do *something.*

Harwinder is the most unhappy—dismissed from her teaching, abandoned by her family, her small eyes, swollen with the tears, magnified behind these thicker and thicker specs. And she was the only one of us to marry for love. What else could we do? We *had* to get her married. She would kill herself, she said, if she could not continue at the university. But the family could not afford her master's, especially in a subject so impractical as English literature. Jeety got her out of India. Jeety was already married at that time to Prakash, an importer of machine parts in the Middle East. He knew every Indian in Aden. But it was Kanwar Singh who bewitched our middle sister with his broad shoulders, heavy-lidded eyes, thick, black beard, and long hair and turban. What attracted Kanwar to our sister, delicate when she was twenty-three, thin and small, like some romantic heroine in the English poems she adored, we will never know. But despite Harwinder's love for English literature, despite even her first love, which no one in the family will ever know, for a Bengali, married professor of English in New Delhi, Harwinder was proud: without anyone arranging a marriage for her, she had found a Khalsa Sikh.

We might have managed to find Baby, the youngest, a husband too, to set our brother up in business and bring the whole family together if the Communists had not nationalized Prakash's business, even Kanwar's import-export. "We must go to England," Harwinder said. "Kanwar can import-export anywhere, and I will enroll in a university."

"What will you do in England?" Kanwar always chided her. "Teach the English how to speak the bloody language they imposed on us? We are Punjabi, if you have not noticed."

"Then we must go back. Even in Delhi I may enroll—"

"Back? I have never *lived* in India! Even my father was born in Kenya."

He was proud. That much our sister and her husband had in common. His mother had a big house in Nairobi. To be sure, in East Africa the Indian community was large. All of the best doctors were Indian. There were Hindu temples, Sikh Gurdwaras, mosques. Grocery stores sold all of our spices, pickles, vegetables, even specialty sweets; restaurants prepared our curries and tandooris; tailors stitched better Punjabi suits than they could stitch in India; Indian jewelers sold twenty-two-carat gold. Though in Africa we dared not wear it— necklaces were snatched, right off ladies' necks; once a burglar tore an earring through Harwinder's earlobe! We were frightened for our sister. Kanwar's house was beautiful, with rooms no one ever used, balconies on which Harwinder served us tea, gardens blossoming with every kind of flower, lawns of pure, green velvet, so thick was the grass that had been tended by the British before they quit Africa. Houseboys brought us everything we wanted; nurses watched the children. But these servants were not such people as we could understand—families with two, three different fathers; they got so angry at the wealth of Indians that they rioted, they beat Indians in the street. And such black faces! In Uganda, just across the border, Africans had thrown the Asians out. We were sure: Harwinder would one day have to leave, with nothing but the clothing on her back, as she and Jeety had no choice but to move out of Aden, as the whole family had fled our home in what is now Pakistan—except our brother, Hari; he was born in Delhi.

The best our sister could do in such a place was teach English in a school for girls—mostly Indians, a few Europeans from the diplomatic corps, and Africans whose fathers were politicians.

"Sister Harvey," Kanwar called her, after *his* teachers, who had all been nuns.

"You are ignorant," she said. "You could never get accepted at a college."

"You call me ignorant!"

We would get a call: Kanwar was not home; Harwinder had been beaten by a burglar; she dared not stay in such an unsafe place. What could we do? Even after the children had been born and were in school, even Harwinder would miss school, she would fly to New Delhi and nurse her breaks and bruises at home.

At first Kanwar would fly across the ocean; and all of us would weep. He was sorry; he would always protect her; he would not allow it to happen again. Prakash would fly in from Bombay and take Kanwar to five-star hotels to drink scotch and discuss: we do not beat our wives, he must control his temper, even if Harwinder *was* emotional; it was her nature, we understood; only he should not drink so much. After a few years—after their daughter had been born—Kanwar would only telephone, demanding that Harwinder return his child: "I will not allow my wife and children to live in her mother-father's house!" Eventually he stopped calling. What was she to do? She *had* to go back to St. Francis' Academy. Children had to go to school. Our brother would do nothing.

"If I go to Nairobi and beat up my brother-in-law," Hari said, "Kenyan police will throw me in an African jail. Is that what you want?"

We told our brother, "You do not have to hit him," though that is precisely what our father had to do when our uncle beat our aunt so many years ago. "Just fetch Harwinder and take her to America."

"What will she do here? She can't work without a green card. How will she live?"

Why do we send our brother cards for our Rakhi holiday for brothers every year if he will not protect us from the families we married into? Was he not raised in the same house? To be sure, our parents sent him to the best of schools, at the family's expense, while our mother kept us sisters together. When Baby failed a subject, even Harwinder dared not admit she had come first in English. But anything Hari did had to be praised. If we did not praise him, our mother said we did not love him. But how could we not love him? He was the darling of the family. He grew tall and strong, a handsome Sikh with his turban and a full, black beard. Though he had no heart. He did nothing when Harwinder's daughter needed us. We had sent the girl to America for college, less than one hour's drive from Hari's house. "I can get Kunti an appointment with the best doctor," he told us. "I will drive her to the clinic myself. She may recover here, as long as it takes to recover from an abortion. But no one can convince that girl not to have the baby."

"Who are you referring to as 'that girl'? She is your own sister's child, your own daughter! How could you leave her alone with a boy? We know what these blacks are like! We have seen them in Nairobi. He may have a child with a different girl for every day of the week. And you would let him force a daughter of this family? Why can you not do for her what we did for Baby twenty years ago?"

And all our brother could say was, "That was in India. And Baby *wanted* the abortion."

Baby was lucky. She got the best husband, though she will never admit—Suraj Singh Arora is the most tolerant man in the family. And after what happened, we were fortunate to find her a husband at all.

Baby was born dark. Her hair, no matter how our mother pulled and oiled it, was coarse and springy, more black than brown. She had a good figure, all of us had figures before the children came, but she was never tall, like Jeety, or delicate and small like Harwinder. She was in between, though she is the youngest. She had never been intelligent enough to study, like Harwinder, and unlike Jeety she did not help our mother with the house. She dressed well; she was good at styling hair. Every morning she tied even Hari's hair, and she was always asked to paint the bride's hands when there was a wedding.

It was the last time all three of us were together in New Delhi. Baby was working in a five-star hotel, styling ladies' hair, painting the nails and giving facials. Harwinder and Jeety were visiting from Nairobi and Bombay. Nitasha had been born, the first of the children. It was before our brother had gone to America, when he was living in the hostel only twenty miles from the house. How would we ever live together? That was all we talked about. Where should we look for a husband for Baby? Not Nairobi. Bombay? One of us should settle in America, our mother said, so that she could make a home for the rest. In America everyone was rich; America never suffered a change of government, would not throw a whole people out just because of their religion or their race. But for some reason Baby did not want to leave. Whenever we mentioned marriage she got angry and ran out onto the street. She was always bursting into tears, refusing to tell us what had made her cry. That was not like Baby. Like Harwinder, maybe, but Baby had never been so emotional. Then one afternoon while we were sitting in the courtyard Hari came home from the college.

"Why are you here so early in the afternoon?" our mother asked. "What about your studies?"

"Holiday," he said, dropping his pack full of heavy books on the concrete floor of the courtyard. "The wedding of the daughter of the dean of engineering."

It was not until the night, after our mother was asleep, that Hari crept into the room where we were sleeping. "Shh! Wake up. It's Baby. Don't tell Biji and Darji"—what we call our mother-father. "No one in the family. It will cost some money."

"Why did she tell *you*?" we asked. "We are her sisters."

Baby burst into crying, but quietly, lest Biji-Darji hear. "How does that matter now?" our brother whispered. "She needs *your* help. *I* can't take her out of Delhi. I can't even find the proper doctor."

How were we to raise a doctor's fee without our husbands knowing? And in India, even in Bombay, everyone would know. "Let me take her to Nairobi," Harwinder said. "She must never see the boy again."

Jeety gave Harwinder as much of her jewelry as could be sold without raising her in-laws' suspicions, and Harwinder took Baby home with her to Nairobi. We had not told anyone, even in the family, yet Baby's secret was discussed from the cousins all the way up to the aunts and uncles. Our mother said, "She will never get a husband now. Thank God you have taken her where she cannot see your father cursing his own blood and denying he ever fathered a third daughter." What were we to do? We had always tried to keep the family together. But fate was pulling us apart.

"Find her a husband in America," our mother said. "So far away, it will not matter."

But we were not so well connected in those days, and we could expect no help from our brother—we were *still* looking for a boy for Baby, even after our brother left New Delhi for New York. Finally the best that we could find was a Nairobi Indian, like Kanwar—except that this Arora, as they called him, was not from our mother-father's region in the Punjab. And he did not wear the turban. He had shaved-off in college in London and settled there. In her grief and shame—which no one would notice after so many months going to parties with Harwinder in Nairobi—Baby agreed to marry him. He was dark-skinned and bald, not at all good looking, and he had reached thirty-two trying to succeed in the hotel business. Finally he sold out to the Arabs, who were overrunning London at that time, and went back to accounting for a multinational corporation. We did not dare send Baby back to India, even for a wedding. Everyone came to Nairobi, except for Hari. As a student he could not afford to fly to Africa, even for the marriage of the last of the sisters. And despite that wild place, in spite of our sister's reputation, the last wedding of the sisters, in the Hotel Intercontinental, turned out beautiful. Even our father wept for joy! Baby, with her down-turned mouth, dark skin and unruly hair, looked like a queen in Harwinder's silks and gold. And our new brother-in-law did not need Kanwar to remind him how to wrap his head in the six yards of pink gauze.

Nothing in her past prevented Baby from giving birth to a son, on her first try, not two years after she had moved to London. Still she complains, and she takes Arora for granted, not realizing how lucky we were to find a man outside of India. None of us likes London. That may be the problem. England is the reason why our brother-in-law calls himself by his last name. It is easier, he says, for these English to remember a word they may have used for these northern lights, what they call them. Baby calls him that, and we got into the habit. What to do? London has gone shabby since the British quit India. It is cold. We must always wear our sweaters. *She* wears wool—pant suits and even dresses, with leggings underneath the skirt, has not worn a sari or even a Punjabi suit since her wedding, and she has cut her hair; it curls up like an English hat around her small, dark face. We can respect the English much more than the Africans; only the young lie about in the streets, dirty and disrespectful. But both places want us out. And why? If it were not for the Indians, Kenya would have nothing, nothing! And were it not for England's

Partition of India and Pakistan, we would never have left our beautiful Punjab. The family would be together.

   Jeety has never been as happy as Baby—she has no house of her
own—though Prakash could never make her as miserable as Kanwar
has made Harwinder. Jeety was the most beautiful of all the sisters.
She could have been a film star if the family were not so shocked at
the very idea of a daughter of the house stared at by so many men.
Her hair grew to the backs of her knees before childbirth and age
thinned and shortened it. It had never been black like Baby's but
brown, straight and silky. All of her features were strong—her eyes
large, her cheekbones sharp and high—and her complexion was as
fair as some of these Americans' whose ancestors migrated from Italy
or Greece. She was the tallest of the sisters but not so tall that she
towered over most men, and though we all had trim and shapely figures before the children, her shoulders were the straightest, her waist
the slimmest, her hips the roundest. It was a wonder she had so
much trouble bearing children.

   The boy that Biji-Darji found for her, Prakash, though he was not
a Sikh, was like a film star too, tall, a little dark but with a firm, strong
jaw and deep brown eyes. Our sister did not mind giving up her job
to keep a house for him in the Middle East—it was by the sea, and
she had a good life. She may have been lonely, but Harwinder went
to stay with her, and after Harwinder was married, there were two of
us together. There may have been three if Jeety had not had to sell all
of the good things her husband had bought for her and move into a
small room in a dark bungalow with the rest of Prakash's family in
Bombay.

   "Jeety! Child! Come!" is the first thing our sister must answer to
every morning, even now. The only room the family could spare

when Prakash brought our sister to Bombay was the room right next to his mother's. And if anything should happen in the night—if Prakash's mother should have any pain or sleeplessness—Jeety must get up and soothe her, bring her water, press her aching bones. Every day after Prakash leaves with his brothers for Sahni's Auto Parts, Jeety gets her mother-in-law out of bed, bathes and dresses her, combs her hair—the poor woman is so arthritic she can no longer lift her arms to coil the bun at the back of her neck.

We know. We have seen her, once the most beautiful of all the sisters, dyeing her hair in secret—thinner now, pulled back into a bun—so that her mother-in-law will not accuse her of trying to make herself look younger so as to attract a younger man! All of her curves have turned to bulges now; her fair skin is dark. She has told us, she has argued with Prakash, nicely, as has always been her way: "Who took care of Mataji before I came?"

"My brothers' wives," he says, in the dark of their room, where he usually falls asleep without even saying goodnight, so tired from twelve hours at the family business.

"Why can they not help me?" she asks, the chatter of the families who had put up shanties in the street, just below their window, shrill and constant, in a language she will never understand.

"My mother loves you best of all the wives. Since you have come into the house, she will have no one else."

And Jeety was so kind, the kindest of the sisters, she could not leave even the cleaning of her mother-in-law's room to the old maid or the houseboy. Whole day she cleaned, cooked. If she wanted something—a sari, even a new blouse—she had to ask Prakash's mother, and then she had better buy all of her sisters-in-law clothing of more or equal value. "Why can't Prakash set up a shop in Delhi?" we asked, we were always asking. "Then you can live with Biji-Darji. We do not believe in this restriction against married daughters living in the house of their mother-father."

But Prakash believed it. The Sahnis were so traditional that they would not even allow the daughters-in-law to work outside the house. "How would it look?" Prakash argued. "As if the Sahnis are not wealthy enough to support the youngest daughter-in-law."

"But if I opened a boutique," Jeety said, "we could afford a flat."

"What is wrong with my father's house? In Aden you complained you were alone."

"Without my family—"

"My family *is* your family."

"We could live anywhere. America. My brother will settle—"

"What can I do in America? In London when I was in college I was nothing but a brown-faced man, third class. Is that the life you want?"

"And why?" her mother-in-law was always asking, before Nitasha had been born, and it was years, four-five years before the first of the children was born. "Why you are not having children? You have been married long enough."

To be sure a son would raise our sister's status in that house. A baby of her own would give her something that no one would want to share, judging from the way her sisters-in-law ignored their own children while the *ayahs* they had hired to look after them chased them around the house. Doctors said she must relax, she must not work too hard. But she came into that house as the youngest; she got all the work. Mataji took her away from the husband who could *get* her a child to consult astrologers, pray at religious shrines. But all she got was Nitasha, dark skinned, self-willed, and besides, a daughter in a house like that could do nothing for the youngest daughter-in-law. Prakash's family believed: daughters are a burden.

We do not agree. We do not believe that girls should leave the family. We are close. We will never love our husbands half so much as we loved our family when we were children, when we were all in India, when we were happy.

"In America," our mother said, "it does not matter. You must send Nitasha there. She can be a doctor. They make lot of money in America. Hari will settle. We will find him a Punjabi lady doctor. *She* will make a house for all of us. The family *must* be together."

What to do? If our brother had only waited for us to find him a Punjabi girl, we might have been welcome in his big house in America. But he informed the family, in a letter to our Jeety, without even asking our advice: he had found his own wife, American.

Jeety flew to Delhi. How could she tell our mother-father on the telephone? What were we to do? The family *had* to discuss our brother's marriage. Jeety flew our mother-father to London. Harwinder met us in Baby's flat. She said, "We cannot allow our brother to marry an American. Think about the children. They will never speak the language. *We* have married men of the same community. We have suffered them to raise our families, though we do not all live in India. Why not our brother?"

"I do not see how we can stop him," Baby said. "If he thinks he loves this girl, then he will marry her, just as you married Kanwar Singh before you considered his education or his nature."

"Who are you to say I did not consider my husband? At least I did not sleep with him until my marriage—"

"I did not sleep with Arora until one full day—"

"Sisters, sisters!" our mother stopped us.

In the end it was Jeety who opened our hearts—it is her nature: "We must go to America. How can we allow our brother to settle so far away, and without the family? He is our brother, and we love him, no matter how he treats the family. We must see that this New Jersey has a university where we can send the children. They *must* make a home for us."

At the airport waiting for our brother to bring the car around, Harwinder's son, Ranjit, only three years old at the time, cried, "I don't like this America," while the most bitter wind we had ever felt cut through our shawls—pure wool; they were nothing in America. Our mother and our father, Jeety and Nitasha, Harwinder and her two (Kunti and Ranjit), and Baby with her Shawn and newborn Sheela—shivered as we tried to fit into Hari's car, so small, though he was in America and could have bought a big American car for all of the family. He had to put Harwinder and Baby and the children in a taxi with the luggage.

His house was big, that was good. But he had no furniture. At least the floors were soft, covered wall to wall. We had the wedding there. We had to. Hari refused to book a five-star hotel. He could not even arrange for a priest to read the holy book. The president of the local Sikh association brought the book. We wrapped the girl in one of our saris. It was the best we could do at such short notice. She was so tall that when she walked around the book her big white feet and ankles stuck out, and without even ankle bracelets or polish on the nails of her long, white toes. Even the children laughed. We had to hush them, covering our smiles. Poor girl, what could she do? She is our only brother's wife. We *must* respect her.

After we had married our brother and ate the holy food we ourselves had cooked, he drove us to a church. Biji wept for fear that the girl might make a Christian out of him while he repeated after the priest that he would stay with this Jill until they both were dead, the white dress that was their custom spreading out so big around her that we thought our brother might be lost.

And so he was.

We tried to love that girl, but she is cold, like her American winters. She does not like us in the house. That is clear, though we tried to teach her how to cook our food, to clean, to look after the children. She took our brother on a honeymoon, and we in America for no more than two months! We do not believe in honeymoons, we told her; the boy's family brings the girl home, and she starts her life. "But this is not your home," she said.

"It is all the same home," we tried to explain, "the same family, the same money," but she will never understand.

She went back to work, in someone else's business. She did not do much; she was not the doctor our mother found for our brother in Delhi. She could take the time off work to take our brother on a honeymoon, but she could not take us shopping. And in America the shopping is so good! Anyone can get anything they want, and cheap. Everyone is so well off, with big houses or at least big cars. Cars sit outside the most run-down of houses. The buses are clean. The roads are kept in good repair. The telephones all work, all the time. Never does the electricity go off, and the water always comes out hot. Americans wear gold, though of an inferior carat, without fear of robbery. This is a place, we saw it with our own eyes, where we thought the children would be safe, rich and happy.

If only our brother would look after them. When Jeety sent Nitasha to America for college, four-five years after we had come to get him married, he put his own niece in a hostel, where Jill could not cook for her and see that she stayed home and studied. Living with Americans, this first girl grew apart from the family. Without our brother's help she could not get into medical school, and he refused for so many years to find a boy for her that now she is too old to get married.

"How do I know she doesn't have a boyfriend?" he asked.

"We are broadminded," Jeety accepted. "We know that the children will choose for themselves. In that case you must talk to the boy. See if he is suitable."

"I don't know if there *is* a boy. Every time I ask her she tells me her love life is none of my business."

"Love life? If she *has* a love life then you *must* see the boy. How can we look out for her? We are not there. You are there, and you will not care for the children."

He would not let Baby's Sheela live with him when Arora could not send her to college. So the girl returned; she will never live in America; she says, "Mum, you just don't know what that country is like. More prejudiced than England even. You will never fit in. And what will you do anyway? You've never worked a day in your life!"

But our sister worked! She was the best at applying marriage make-up in all of Delhi! In America she could own her own beauty parlor. Jeety could open a boutique. Harwinder could start her own school.

Must the family *only* come together when somebody dies? The last time we were all together we immersed our father's ashes in that cold, gray water that separates New York from the Statue of Liberty. And in a country with the best medical care in the world, so poorly did our brother look after him! There we stood, freezing with the cold, layers of fat hiding Jeety's beauty, Harwinder no longer able to remember those mysterious lines of the English poet that had stirred her so when she had been Dr. Rabindra Bose's best student:

'Tis dark: quick pattereth the flaw-blown sleet:
"This is no dream, my bride, my Madeline!"
'Tis dark: the iced gusts still rave and beat:
"No dream, alas! Alas! And woe is mine!

Baby has lost weight in England, and she wears her hair too short for her small, dark face. She was the only sister brave enough to grab our mother's hands when our mother beat her own chest, shouting at our father's body, "What did I do to you that you must make your wife a widow at this age and in this place?"

Hari tells us we must let go of the past. But how are we to live, even for the present, when the children are not settled? It is our duty to educate the children, get them married, in good families, and well off. *For the children,* we correct our brother, *we have always lived for the future, not the past.*

We have consulted astrologers on four continents! The predictions have not all come true, but that is because the exact times of our births were forgotten when the family fled Pakistan. Harwinder must wear an opal on the first finger of her right hand to insure that Kanwar will treat her kindly. All of us eat only vegetarian on Tuesdays. With better fortune, the children will settle; we will join them in America.

Our mother comforts us, when we come to visit her in Hari's house in California, where he has moved, far across the country from the children: "Prakash *must* retire. When his only child is settled he will come. And if he does not, what can you do? Leave him with his precious Bombay family. Arora *must* come. All of his family are here. As for Harwinder, we just have to wait until that black who got Kunti pregnant leaves her for another woman. He will, when he gets another child. Then we will find her a husband. Widower, divorcé, what does it matter? So long as he is able to support her and willing to support the child with his own. What does a girl have if she does not have a husband? Her brother will come for her wedding—you can get anything for weddings in this country, saris, jewelry, even the five-star hotel—and we will force him to stay. Without his motorcycle he will find a job, he might even go to college. People go to college at all ages in America. Even Harwinder can complete her master's, as she always wanted."

None of us believe that even *she* believes that Nitasha will ever get married, let alone Kunti. And yet they must. And our mother *must* be consoled. How can a daughter argue with her dying mother?

Someone said, perhaps one of our astrologers, that our suffering in this life may provide some happiness a hundred years from now. For our children's children. When we are forgotten. But they *must* remember us. They must bless us for the way we tried. Or he was referring to our next lives. They *must* be happy. Only we must live in this life. We must work. Everyone works in America. It is the work ethic. Hari has said: *What will you do? You will have to work in America.* We know. We have worked. All of our lives we have only fulfilled our duty to the children. If only we knew the exact times when we had been born. Then the astrologers could tell us where we must go, where we will be. If only we knew. If we only knew.

9 Double Mind

Nitasha Sahni
Jersey City, New Jersey

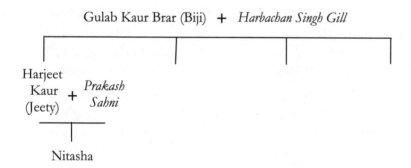

Gulab Kaur Brar (Biji) + *Harbachan Singh Gill*

Harjeet Kaur (Jeety) + *Prakash Sahni*

Nitasha

W HEN MY MOTHER came from Mumbai, which was called Bombay when I grew up there, to visit me and my grand-mother and uncle, where they are living now, in California, she brought a list of names and numbers—the boys I finally agreed to meet with prospects of marriage. The first was a Wall Street banker, who hadn't had the time, as he explained it, between working twelve-hour days and going for his MBA, either to sustain a relationship in New York or fly to India to see some girls.

The way he phrased it, "see some girls," turned my stomach. I couldn't look at anything but the moussaka I had ordered in the downtown restaurant, where my mother and I had met him. And all I could see in the eggplant and the cheese was short, plump Arun Batra sitting cross-legged on his mother's bed, in new, starched cotton pa-jamas from a cottage industries emporium explaining, "Yes, I saw the girl. She is dark. She is not a doctor. She is almost thirty years old."

I had resisted being "shown," as my family called it, ever since my graduation from Rutgers University. One of my most vivid memories is hiding in the curtains hanging in the doorway of the drawing room of the Bombay house where I grew up, giggling with my best friend since first grade, Lalita Das. On the other side my older cousins sat wrapped up in gaudy silks they could hardly walk in, let alone run away in, their heads bowed miserably as the families of the men who were considering them for marriage threw back and forth at one another, "A degree in French?" Or English. Or Music. "We speak Punjabi, if you have not noticed. We do not allow our girls to sing outside the home." And "She is skinny. Marriage will put fat on her. Before I had children . . ."

"I'm not ever getting married," Lalita always said, dashing into the garden, where we preferred kicking my cousins' footballs and climbing trees to playing with the dolls my aunts brought me from England, dressing up the way our mothers loved to do, or helping the cooks cut fresh beans for dinner.

"When we grow up we'll go to America," I used to say. "We'll be businesswomen in New York."

When we were teenagers, we laughed at our classmates' obsessions with film stars or worse, real boys. My grandmother used to pad onto the veranda where we always studied and say, "Comb your hair." Once she eyed Lalita suspiciously and pronounced, "You will never get a husband if you do not slim down."

We laughed until we cried, me ruffling Lalita's curls I loved so much, she tickling me until I almost wet the white cotton pants beneath the plaid skirt of my school uniform. When we were back, quiet, hunched over our books again, she asked, "Am I fat? Should I give up sweets?"

"I love chocolate," I moaned.

"You don't love me?"

After I had come to America, I missed her so much I could barely wait for my first summer holiday. My miserly American aunt noticed the length of my calls and suggested I write instead. But how could I put my innermost thoughts into a letter anyone might find and read? How could I be cheered up by Lalita's witty quips if I could not talk to her? Then, before my semester ended, her family immigrated to Canada—the sudden culmination of a long-term plan, like my mother's dream to live with me in America. Lalita came to see me even before her family was settled in.

We had so much to talk about. "Americans are so obsessed with sex," I told her. "Boys and girls pair up before they even know each other. They get serious—"

"Eight months in America and you're an expert on boys," she teased, striding ahead of me down Albany Street. I liked to stand against the parapet of the Raritan bridge and stare into the wide, slow-moving river. Its muddy bed poking through the shallow water reminded me of the Jumna in New Delhi, where my mother had been raised, where *her* mother still had a house, still stayed when she wasn't visiting one of my aunts or living in New Jersey with my uncle, aunt and cousin.

"I dated once," I said. "Only once. I should have known I was out of my element when I couldn't get my roommate to go with us. God, in India my entire house full of cousins goes on dates together! 'Are you kidding?' she said. 'Bob asked you.' All the way back from the movie—in which I had to watch a couple doing it—"

"Chee!"

"—I tried to start a conversation. Nothing. Then he thought he could kiss me!"

"Disgusting!"

"He was not unattractive—hair the color of sand, but with the kind of deep, brown eyes I—"

She sang, "Nitasha is in love."

I pushed her, laughing. "If a person won't say one word, how do you know if you even like him? He asked me out again, but I won't go."

Lalita put her arm around me as we crossed the flat bridge over the steep, high banks. Below us the trees were just coming into leaf, some of them still in blossom; the water was flowing for a change, covering its muddy islands. "So I don't have to worry about attending your wedding any time soon," she concluded.

"Are you kidding?"

I didn't even see the need for a boyfriend. My roommates, on the other hand, like most Americans, spent so much time chasing the opposite sex that they have no time for real communication.

I spent my first three summers in India, with no one to talk to. My cousins were all away at school, married or making money in England, the Middle East, even India. Lalita's family could not afford to send her, and besides, she had no one left in India but her aunts. They could never deal with her refusal to exchange her jeans for saris and salwar kameezes as her cousins, even my cousins had. They got on her nerves, like my grandmother on my father's side, who kept nagging my mother to bring me some prospective husbands. People were always arguing right in front of me as if I wasn't there: "The girl is old enough to get married, a rich family will support her better than a college degree halfway across the world!"

"You must not blame your grandmother," my mother reminded me, about my father's mother, whom we lived with in Bombay. "She herself was married at fourteen. There was no other way." Besides, I did not know it at the time, but Mum was right. When I finished my degree, I fantasized, I'd get a job and bring my mother and father over, even my annoying grandmother. I never got that job—that is, well paying enough to allow me to support them. I could not even support myself. But in my second year of college the rest of my life was the farthest thing from my mind. I stopped spending every weekend and holiday with my mother's brother, his family, and my mother's mother, who all lived just a half-hour's drive away from my dormitory, and went to see Lalita and her mother, father and brother in Canada. And every chance she got she came to see me at Rutgers. Lonely weeks between passed quickly when I knew that soon I would be able to talk all night with someone who actually listened, someone who knew me better than anyone else on earth. I went out some weekends with the one or two girls in my dormitory who were not obsessed with going out with boys, but other than that I had to wait for Lalita.

It was not until the summer between my sophomore and junior years, back in India for my annual visit, that I heard the rumor I had not heard in America.

My father lost no time, on the drive home from the airport, stalled between a rattling lorry and a camel laden with textiles: "You are not to see that dirty girl again. People talk. Whether she is behaving improperly—"

"What girl?"

"You know what girl. That Das, something."

"Lalita? Improper?" Beggars tapped on the window of my father's Mercedes as I leaned over the back of the front seat and tried to explain, "Americans are so obsessed with sex—"

"This was no American who told your mother you were seen fooling with that—"

"It was Sanjay!"

"Who is Sanjay?" Mummy asked, pulling me back into the seat, to face her where she sat beside me, while my luggage rode up front with Daddy.

"A boy I met in the Indian Student Association. He told everyone the reason I would not go out with him is I have a boyfriend at Hari Uncle's house."

"Who is this boyfriend, child? At Hari's? Is he Indian?"

"I don't *have* a boyfriend! It's a lie. And you want me to betray my best friend just because the Indian Student Association saw me hug her—"

"Okay, okay," my mother said, closing her hand over mine. She leaned forward to talk to my father. "Why we are spreading this gossip? It is as I said: they are like sisters, these girls."

"She has cousin-sisters," my father retorted. "What is so bad about family that a girl must have these friends?"

Lalita and I had never kept a secret, but I couldn't tell her. I was afraid to hurt her feelings. She was not attractive in a conventional way, but neither did I have the light, rosy complexion valued by families wishing to lighten up the next generation. I was slim though, even by American standards, and my hair was straight; I had never cut it. Lalita loved it, envied it, I sometimes thought, as I loved her wild curly mop.

But that did not mean Lalita and I were doing anything my father was afraid of. I wasn't doing anything with anybody. Maybe in my dreams. Nightmares frightened me. Once I dreamed that I was standing in the shower. I turned, and there was Lalita, the water straightening her hair, her breasts pressed up against me, large and full, like the breasts of the carvings of the goddesses on temple walls I'd seen in India. She kept repeating, "Do you want to?" I woke up, my heart pounding. It was not always Lalita in those dreams, not ever a woman when it wasn't her. My older cousins did things they never did in life, though we had grown up together in the same joint household, sometimes sleeping in the same room, the same bed. After I had come to the United States I woke up thinking that my uncle—twenty years older than me, my mother's baby brother—had just rolled off of me onto the floor of the drawing room of Sahni House, where he had never been. My breath caught, my heart beat as if to burst.

I was terrified. I could remember learning about penance from the nuns, my teachers in Bombay. My mother will never know why, sometimes, I would not allow the servant to put sugar in my tea. Then in Psychology at Rutgers I read Freud. Could dreams express the fears we feel in our unconscious minds? I would be the first to admit I was afraid of anyone touching me the way that I felt touched in those dreams.

So when my parents brought up marriage, on my college graduation, I was so embarrassed that I lost my temper. We were standing—my mother, my father, my mother's mother, and me—in my uncle Hari's guest room. Suitcases lay open on the twin beds my grandmother and grandfather slept in, the clothing, knick-knacks and household items my mother had brought spread out on top of my father's shirts and my mother's bright salwar kameezes. "Why you brought all this?" my father complained, in that low growl his voice had aged to. "As she did not get acceptance to the medical school, she must come back to India and meet some boys."

I can still remember the rush of panic I felt when I said, "I cannot be*lieve* you would try to marry me off. Just because I don't want to be a doctor." Tears of anger filled my eyes.

"No, no, she must stay," my mother said, her hands, as usual, reaching out to soothe and comfort me. "She must settle in America."

"We must find her an Indian boy living in this country," my grandmother said.

"I don't want a boy," I cried, "living anywhere! God! Even in India you worked before she found you a husband."

Bringing up my grandparents' arrangement of my parents' marriage embarrassed all three of them. They did not mention marriage again—until the years had passed, I got tired of working, and I told my mother that I didn't want to be single for the rest of my life, didn't want to get too old to have a child, and had not met anyone that I could marry.

It was after my cousin, my mother's sister's daughter, Kunti, had given birth to a beautiful baby girl. The first time I saw her, tears blurred the lights inside the nursery and my palms turned cold against the glass that separated visitors from newborns. She was fast asleep, her black hair thick and curly, her color pure honey. How I longed to hold her. When I did, a few nights later, at the apartment I'd moved out of after my cousin had invited the baby's father to move in, I realized I would rather die than never hold a baby of my own. The father was out, I don't know where he was, I could never stand him, never could stand any of my cousin's boyfriends. Kunti, three years younger than I, stood hovering over my shoulder, smelling sour, wrapped in a thin dressing gown in need of washing. "She gives *so* much trouble. I have not slept for two hours together."

On the train back to Jersey City my arms ached as if I'd lifted something so much heavier than myself that my muscles would not ever lose their knots. I began to think that to have babies even an arranged marriage might be preferable to the destruction Kunti worked on her family by giving birth out of wedlock. Despite the distance, when my aunt's headmistress in Nairobi found out that her strictest teacher had become the grandmother of an illegitimate, black granddaughter, she asked Harwinder Massi, as we call our mother's sister in India, to resign. Even Kunti's father lost business, though to be honest, he was not much better—he drank, he was abusive, he even had a mistress. If I had given birth to a child without a proper, Indian wedding, *my* family would throw my parents out of Sahni House. And how would they live with me in the one room I had moved to in Jersey City? I didn't make enough even to support myself.

Lalita was always quick to remind me, "In order to have babies, you will have to do what your cousin does."

"Have you ever done it?" I asked Lalita, knowing without asking that she would have told me if she had.

"This is not about me," she said. "This is about you getting married to fill up your apartment. What will you do when he's produced those babies, and you can't find another use for him?"

"Lala, that is cruel. Don't you ever want a family?"

It was easier for her. She was lucky. After she had graduated with a worthless degree in South Asian Studies, her parents bought her a business. She was always offering to share it with me: "Give up America. Come to Niagara Falls and help me manage this motel."

Without permanent residence in the United States, I had to settle for an internship—not a medical internship, a student internship in hospital administration. Lucky for me it turned into a job, illegal and dead-end even before I started, but better, far better, than tracking down the partners of VD patients or checking up on welfare recipients—what my fellow sociology majors all seemed to be doing. Graduate school was out of the question. I didn't have the energy; besides, Mummy and Daddy would never be able to convince the family to pay any more tuition unless I could somehow change my mediocre grades and convince the American Medical Association to raise their limits on foreign students. I still took my vacations with Lalita, but she had to come to me. I might get a visa for Canada, but my student visa to the United States had expired. If I went to Canada, immigration officials might not allow me back.

"I can't do that to my mother." I always refused Lalita's offer. "She sent me here to settle."

"Here is not Canada?"

"Canada is cold," I said, even New Jersey was colder than my parents were used to, but my grandmother had brainwashed my mother into setting her sights on living in the same state as my uncle. That was before my uncle thwarted all of the family's plans and moved to California.

"I'll sell Niagara Nivas," Lalita offered, "buy us a bed and breakfast in Vancouver."

Just the words "bed and breakfast," and I could not help but remember the yellow and white wood house we stayed in on a trip we took to Florida. Lalita was always willing to drive, on her January trips, to places she wanted to see—Washington DC, Disney World, Key West. My face burned at the memory of waking in the middle of the night to a rhythmic falsetto gasp, "Oh, oh, oh!"

I had to force my voice out of sleep. "Someone's hurt."

Chuckling Lalita rolled to my side of the bed and put her arm around me, the way we often woke on my futon in Jersey City. She mumbled into my hair, "Men can really hurt each other when they do it."

I held my breath listening to those men catch their breaths in the room next door. When I let it out, it came in giggles. Lalita dug her fingertips into my ribs. "Stop," I said. "Stop," laughing so hard I could not roll over to retaliate. Tears ran down my face. I fell off the bed and just made it into the bathroom. The fan drowned out the sound of the men next door. When I turned it off, the place was silent.

"Climax," Lalita said, stretched out in the middle of the bed, smiling, her hair all over the pillow. "You missed it."

"Men are animals," I said, crawling in beside her. She nodded, still listening, I thought, her eyes not focused on anything. "Move," I said. "God, you hog the bed!"

She looked at me as if she were thinking of tickling me again. "Don't you dare," I said, my hands raised to attack the soft flesh at her midriff. She didn't move. Then she got up and went into the bathroom. I wondered why she was taking a shower in the middle of the night, but I fell asleep before I got a chance to ask.

I had always been disgusted at the very thought of touching someone else's naked body, letting someone touch what even I had always been shy about touching. Maybe Lalita knew that, even before that embarrassing night. I told her how my younger cousin nauseated me with the sounds she and her boyfriend made, whatever boyfriend she was seeing, on the floor of our drawing room, while I tried to sleep in the bedroom we usually shared. I had been happy, during my senior year, to move out of a cheap apartment with four friends—all of whom were boring me with stories of their boyfriends anyway, past, present, and future—to take care of my cousin for my aunt Harwinder, her mother, my mother's sister. "How do you need roommates?" Harwinder Massi asked me. "You have family. If your uncle would buy you a car, you could live in his house and drive to the university. But my brother has never supported the family. At least you must live with your cousin. It is your duty to protect her from the influence of these Americans."

If she had only known, my cousin had lost her innocence even before leaving Africa. On Kunti's first weekend in our new apartment, a boy who had lived next door to her in Nairobi drove out from Purdue, Indiana and slept with her—loudly—on the floor of our living room, just outside the bedroom door. I might have been able to get used to Kabir—I liked him, he was quiet, sensitive, though I hated that sound, like someone being beaten—but when he went back to Indiana, Kunti brought home other guys. I didn't move out until after she graduated—family pressure; I'd thought it was family loyalty at the time. Then she went too far and asked a homeless guy to live with us. He was still there, the father of her baby—family, American style. I moved to a studio in Jersey City, just across the river from New York. It was there Lalita asked me, lying on the wall-to-wall in front of my floor to ceiling window, looking out across the gray Hudson at the even grayer skyline of Manhattan, "Do me a favor. Don't let your parents fix you up with the typical Indian boy."

"Why not? On my own I haven't managed to meet even the atypical *American* boy."

"Because you wouldn't be able to stand living with a boy—either Indian or American."

"Don't be stupid. I grew up in a house full of boys."

"A husband is hardly the same thing as a cousin," she said. "Trust me, 'Tash. I know you better than you know yourself."

That may have been true. But I saw no way to improve my wretched life unless I could meet someone who did not make me feel as if I were being led into a deep, dark tunnel from which I would never escape.

Mummy invited Baldev, a research scientist at Johnson & Johnson, and cooked her famous *biriyani*, but I could not bring myself to imagine his pug face across the table from me every day. We met Charanjit at his mother's restaurant in Manhattan. I objected: "I said I didn't want to meet anybody who's living with his mother."

"She is so modern," Mummy said. "Look how she is wearing a dress!"

"With leggings," like the churidar trousers my mother used to wear beneath her long, dress-like kameezes, until her calves got too fat and she preferred to cover them with wide, baggy salwars.

Not all of the "boys" my mother called were interested in marrying a twenty-nine-year-old without a high-paying job. I wondered how many were interested in arranging a marriage at all. Divorcés and widowers with kids were out. I wanted a baby of my own, not somebody else's.

"Okay, let me call the boys between New York and California. If they say that they would like to meet you, we will break our trip."

"Mummy, it costs a lot to make a stop-over voluntarily."

"I have come too far to miss one boy just because he may not live in New York or California."

"What about where *I* live?" I said. "Doesn't that matter?"

But the only prospect willing to meet us lived in Cleveland. If I moved there, I consoled myself, I could drive to Niagara Falls whenever I needed a laugh, some understanding. Was I so wrong to want an authentic life? With an engineer's income I might even buy a car, as consolation for everything he would expect me to do.

I called Lalita from the Ritz Carlton, where my uncle had booked Mum and me a room. "Drive down for the night," I suggested. "We've got two double beds."

"Won't I interfere with the process of 'bride viewing'?" she asked, with more than the usual sarcasm.

"Don't the sisters of the family get to 'see' the boy? We're meeting him downstairs in the bar. Look for us there."

When I hung up, happy that my best friend would be on hand to assess at least one prospect, Mummy said, "It is not good to ask her to the first meeting with this boy."

"He'll have to meet her sooner or later," I said, "if this one goes beyond one date."

"Later is another thing," she said. "First impression is very important."

"Are you saying that Lalita might create a negative impression?"

"She wears *only* jeans."

"I've worn jeans," I reminded her, "for all three of my dates."

"But you are not like her."

"Then there isn't any problem."

"Child," she said. "So far you have not liked even one boy. What will you do if you like this one and he judges you because your friend—"

"I will not marry a man who wants to isolate me from my friends. God, Mummy, were you ever happy, the way Daddy's family tried to separate you from your sisters—"

"No one can separate the sisters."

John (formerly Gian) was already in the bar when we came down. He was by far the best looking of all the prospects, with sharp, strong features and a wave of thick black hair. I was beginning to think I might be attracted to one of these boys. He had a PhD from Case Western and had worked for BP America long enough to qualify for a pension. Secretly I hoped he would say nothing embarrassing and that his mother and father were dead. He ordered another scotch and soda and a glass of wine for me, for Mummy a Coke.

We talked about Bombay—our schools, our families, the beaches. We had a lot in common. Then we moved on to our colleges. At that point Mummy slipped into listening and John ordered a third scotch. "Would you care for another?"

"One's my limit," I said, automatically putting my hand over my glass.

"Oh," he said. "Cheap drunk."

Whatever attraction I might have had slipped away as the ice in Mummy's second Coke turned to water. He must have been a party boy, who had been afraid to upset his family by introducing them to his American girlfriend. On the up side, he seemed more laid back than the boys I'd met in New York—it's true what they say about the Midwest—flexible hours, except when they were working on a project. In his free time he went sailing on the lake. He ordered another scotch.

"I think maybe we should eat little bit," Mummy said, pushing her bulk up off the chair. John held up his hand, stood up—a bit unsteadily, I thought—swaggered to the bar and brought back a fifth scotch and a bowl of pretzels.

Mummy sat down as he did, picked up a pretzel and stared at it as if she were trying to decide whether to kill her hunger or destroy my chances by telling John he drinks too much.

"Funny thing about those pretzels," John said, slurring dangerously. "Shaped like an Indian sweet, but—"

"They are nothing more than hard bread and salt," my mother finished, looking up from the pretzel with a frown. I twisted around in my chair to see what she was looking at. Lalita stood at the entrance to the bar, her hair wild, as usual, about her round, dark face, wearing the baggy jeans—my mother was right—she always wore, and a puffy red down parka over a man's plaid flannel shirt open over one of the Niagara Falls T-shirts she sold at the motel. I stood up and ran to her.

"This is my best friend, Lalita Das," I told John, having walked her to the table arm in arm.

He looked up, his eyelids heavy. "John Bharsatti," he said, aiming his hand in Lalita's direction. "Buy you a drink?"

Lalita laughed.

"I think we have had enough," Mummy said, rising from the chair and rubbing Lalita on one shoulder blade in greeting. "You must eat," she told John, "or you will not be able to drive."

"No problem," he said. "I do it all the time. I have a Merc. It literally drives itself."

I convinced Mummy that I was too tired to sit through dinner. We ordered sandwiches and ate upstairs in our room, my mother worried that John might wrap his Mercedes around an innocent victim on a Cleveland freeway. Lalita and I could not stop laughing. "Have they all been drunks?" she asked. "Or were some of them sober assholes?"

"Sober assholes."

"Girls," my mother said, "it is not a way for ladies to speak."

"Not much sperm in an alcoholic," Lalita muttered.

I was laughing too much to be shocked.

"You must sleep," my mother said. "We must fly to California in the morning. And Lalita has a long drive, isn't it?"

We changed into our pajamas, and Lalita and I climbed into one of the queen-sized beds.

"I will sleep with Nitasha," my mother said.

"We're used to sharing," I said.

Lalita was finding it hard to control her laughter, as if *she* had drunk John's scotch.

"She is our guest," my mother said. "We must not disturb."

"She won't be disturbed."

"It's okay, Auntie," Lalita said. "We'll be good."

I frowned at my mother, and she crawled reluctantly into the empty bed, looking at us the doubtful way she used to look at me whenever I got into an argument with family. Under the covers Lalita pulled my arm across her waist. I exhausted myself holding in my laughter. Waiting for my mother to fall asleep, I dozed. Lalita woke me, her breath blowing warmly in my ear. "'Tash," she was calling me, "'Tasha."

"Wha—"

"Don't go through with it. Don't get married."

I sighed, rolled onto my back, my right arm pressing up against her large, soft breast. "I have doubts myself," I whispered. "Who wouldn't, considering what's left."

"I'm what's left," she said. "At least I will be if you leave me for one of these losers."

"No, you won't." When she didn't answer I rolled onto my side and draped one arm around her. She put her hands on my hips, pulled me closer. Then I felt her lips on my neck. "Lala?" I said.

She kissed me on the shoulder, slipped downward in the bed, her warm lips grazing the skin where my pajama top fell open. "Lalita!" I said, slipping more than pushing her away.

"Girls?" my mother said.

Lalita looked up, the whites of her eyes glowing in the light thrown off by the face of the clock radio between the beds. How were we to talk about it now, my mother in the room not ten feet away?

I moved my mouth as close as possible to Lalita's ear. "Is it true?" I asked in my most quiet whisper. "Do you—"

"Do I love you?"

"Girls!"

I lay on my back staring at the ceiling until my mother's breathing seemed more regular, but I could not fall asleep until I knew: "How long have you known?"

"Haven't you ever wondered why you never put posters of Tom Cruise or Amitabh Bachan on your walls?"

"At Sahni House? Never!"

"Or why you loved my painting of Krishna's milk maids, the way the painter stopped their blouses halfway down those bulging breasts."

"Those are religious paintings!"

"Children, if you cannot sleep, I must change places," my mother said, sitting up to take Lalita's place.

"No," I said. "We'll sleep."

But I could not sleep. What if Lalita was right? If I had never fallen in love not because the boys were so crude and boring but because I was not attracted to boys in the first place? But I was not attracted to women either. When had she turned gay, I wondered; had all of those times we'd rolled on the veranda of Sahni House, tickling, all those times she plaited my hair—had they been a kind of foreplay neither one of us had known how to escalate into the things my best friend must have learned in college? Or had she known? I wondered how much noise she and I might make getting dressed to sneak out of the room, down to the bar again, where we could talk. But John might still be there. Or some man might come up and start a conversation, like the men who had tried to pick us up once or twice in New Brunswick.

I whispered, "Why didn't you tell me?"

I could feel the mattress wobble as she shrugged. "How could I? I was cheating on you."

"Cheating?"

"Every time."

"Lala," I said. "I'm not—"

"That's not important," she said. "Do you love me?"

"I—yes." There had never been any question. Hadn't I said it to myself, all the time?

My mother shifted, and neither of us dared to speak again or even move for fear that she might kick Lalita out, and not just out of bed. I don't think any of us slept all night. At first light we got up, showered and dressed. Lalita drove us to the airport. How could we talk with Mummy in the car, herself silent? Lalita hugged us both and promised to drive to Jersey City after New Year's, as usual.

If I could have borne the thought of hurting my mother, if I'd ever been capable of doing anything my heart told me to do, I would have put Mummy on the plane and stayed in the car with Lalita. But I knew my mother would have whimpered all the way to San Francisco, even without me to hear it. She would have gotten off the plane and clung to my grandmother, tears rolling down her face. Then, while Mummy hugged my uncle, my grandmother would widen her cloudy eyes, raise her hands and pretend to look for me around the crowded gate. Mummy would have to dream up some lie—that I could not get two weeks off—in order to avoid telling them that I had gone off to Canada with "that girl."

I did not even have the time to explain it to my mother before boarding the plane, elbow to elbow with strangers, with secrets of their own. I'm not sure I even understood myself. And though I sat beside her for five hours I couldn't talk. How much had she heard, I wondered; how much had she understood? We watched the movie, ate what we could of the insipid lunch the cabin attendants dropped onto our tray tables, and spoke, when we spoke at all, of irrelevant matters.

"That girl—Lalita—has put on little weight. She doesn't try to slim down?"

"Everybody eventually puts on weight," I said, pressed between my mother's broad hip and the even broader American hip of the woman wedged into the window seat beside me.

To be sure, my grandmother had come to the airport with my uncle. Ten years younger than my father's mother, this grandmother had a different look entirely. She carried her weight in front of her, like a pregnancy. She dyed her hair, brown, not black, and wore the brightest, latest in Delhi salwar kameezes, as if she couldn't bear to admit that her oldest granddaughter was almost thirty. She had seen so many changes in her life—the loss of her ancestral lands, the modernization of the city she was forced to live in when she had to leave those lands, her children spread out all over the world—that I could understand her expectations. She insisted that my mother and her sisters support each other, though they lived thousands of miles apart. She put pressure on my uncle to support us all, and he worked day and night to accumulate enough to give thousands to anyone his mother asked him to give it to, though that was hardly ever me. That the whole family—sisters, brother, kids—would one day live in California in Hari Uncle's million-dollar house was her fondest, most impossible dream. But who would want to live in her uncle's house, working, no doubt, in her uncle's Midas Muffler franchise, counting the months before she could fly back east and have a genuine conversation with her best friend in the world?

"So, you have come to meet some boys," she said, patting me on a shoulder blade as she hobbled onto the moving walkway that led to the baggage pick-up.

"No, Biji," I said. "I have come to see you and Hari Uncle."

"Good girl," she said, smiling at my mother. "Good family girl." Then she got down to business, leaning on my mother's arm. "Your brother does not know any Indians. I have had to call the cousins in Los Angeles. They know every Indian in California. We will go there in the weekend, stay one week or two—"

"I've only got two weeks," I said.

"I have the names of two-three boys in San Francisco," my mother said. "We will call them and—"

"I can't go through any more blind dates," I said.

"But we have come to—"

"There's nothing left, Mummy. Misfits, drunks and mama's boys." Besides, I could not go on with any of this farce until I spoke to Lalita.

I let my mother and grandmother talk, scheming, I thought, to contact the boys on my mother's list, then present me with an offer I could not refuse: income that would buy me anything I wanted for the rest of my life; meaningful work if I wanted it, fulfilling leisure if I did not; a family as nurturing and satisfying as the family I had left in India. All of that would come attached, however, to the price tag of an interfering husband and his family. I wished I could have found the privacy in my uncle's house to call Lalita. But my aunt Jill followed me from room to room, asking me how I was doing in New Jersey, was it cold there, was my job all right, was I looking for another job, how was Kunti, was my friend still in Canada?

"Yes," I said, "yes, yes, yes," and all the time I was wasting in California I kept wondering: had Lalita told her parents? How would she live for the rest of her life? Alone? With lovers? Had she *had* a lover? How many lovers had she had? Why had she not told me? I felt such aching in my chest that I stayed up late one night when everyone else had gone to bed, despite my mother's insistence that I sleep, "Sleep. You will be so tired in the morning." But just as I picked up the phone, I heard the kitchen door open, and my cousin Rosa walked in. "You're home late," I said.

She put a finger, the nail a bright blue, to her lips. "Rosie?" her father called, from his bedroom upstairs.

"Shit," she said. "I can't do anything in this house without the whole world knowing about it."

In the morning I came into the kitchen when my mother was dialing the phone. "Who are you calling?" I asked.

"Oh," she said, hanging up before she could complete the call. "That Rajan, the son of your father's friend, who grew up in London."

"Mummy, I said I don't want to meet any more boys."

"But why, child? You are here for two weeks only."

"I can't explain it. I just can't bear the thought of going out on a blind date with any more of these misfits. I'm beginning to think I'm a misfit myself."

"You are not a misfit," she said, smoothing my long hair behind my back. "You are a beautiful, intelligent girl. This boy will like you, you will see."

"But will I like him? That's more important."

"That is important," she agreed. "But not so important in the beginning."

"Then when *is* it important?"

"For the rest of your life, child."

The rest of my life. That was the problem.

Hari Uncle drove us down the coast, taking a long, long route so he could show us Monterey, the Big Sur, scenery beautiful enough almost to justify living in California, though Lalita would not be able to drive all the way from Niagara Falls even once a year. She and I had never taken a vacation in the west, but watching the Pacific pass, remembering the west coast of India, I wished we had, wished she were there with me, alone in the car, so that I could tell her *Lala, I can't stand it anymore. What shall I do? Go back to the only home I've ever loved and put up with my father's family's resentment of the burden I am as a single woman unable to support myself? Or move to your cold tourist trap until I hate that too?*

I thought I knew what she would say, and it made my heart race, as it had pounded when I heard Arun say "see some girls," when I caught my mother trying to call San Francisco, when Lalita kissed my breast and said, "How could I tell you? I was cheating."

The LA cousins really did know every Indian in California. I heard cousin Pinky whispering to cousin Preetie, who in turn whispered to her friend, Bubbly, who all whispered with my mother: "What about the Mehra's son in San Luis Obispo?"

"The Mehra's son? Oh, he is only twenty-five."

"Twenty-five? Not thirty-five?"

"Well, then, Saroj's cousin's son, what is his name?"

"He is living with a girl for the past two years. It is a scandal. Unless they made him move back home to San Diego. If they make him give her up, then—"

I told my mother, "Make them stop. Make them, or I will."

After a week of talk, no boys in sight, despite the dinner parties— all married couples, with excellent recipes and a range of overactive, obnoxious children—Mummy, my grandmother and I caught a commuter flight back to San Francisco. Mummy would stay with my grandmother and uncle. I had to get back to the hospital, unless I wanted to be fired and make it even more necessary to marry for a Green Card and money. But before I could fly back, my father called from Bombay. "So? No boys were good? There is still that Rajan. His father, my friend, called all the way from London to ask me what we thought. What could I say? You have not seen the boy. And you are so close. At least you must call him. It is not so far. Look him up at his office. You have the number. You cannot travel so far, spending the family money, then not see the one boy who might be suitable."

"I will not be able to face your father or his family if I do not call," Mummy said.

And I remembered the arguments she'd had with my father's family, one evening in particular when Daddy's brothers summoned both of us—my mother and me—into the drawing room. For an hour they asked the stupidest questions about Rutgers University, which I knew nothing about before I had begun my first semester. Was I intelligent enough to study medicine, how long would it be before I could be earning one-hundred thousand dollars a year? Four years later when the family found out I had no intention of going to medical school, I was too far away to be summoned. Mummy never told me how much she'd been faulted for raising me to have a mind of my own. But they had never thought much of her for having only one child in the first place, and at that a daughter.

"Okay, call him," I said. "But I won't go out with him."

"Child, what am I to say if he agrees to meet us?"

"You might not have to say anything," I said. I grabbed the receiver. Get it over with, I thought, and then even if I had to have lunch with the guy, Mummy could tell Daddy I had tried. And *I* could tell him that the dark skin I had inherited from him had made me unmarketable, even as the family's money set the trap.

A man answered, with an English accent: "Roger Hallowell."

"May I speak to Rajan Ahluwalia," I asked, reading the name off Mummy's list.

There was a pause. "Who may I say is calling?"

"My name is Nitasha Sahni," I said, in my best hospital voice. "I'm visiting from New York. My father went to college in London with Rajan Ahluwalia's father."

The voice on the other end of the line produced a peal of light, spontaneous laughter. "I call myself Roger."

Not another one, I thought. "Hallowell?"

"I have enough trouble protecting my privacy," he said, the *i* short and not unsweet, "without a surname that provokes people to poke into my ethnic background."

Englishman, I thought, and despite my better judgment I liked Rajan/Roger's tone; his voice, deep but with lighter inflections, reminded me of Lalita's. "That may be as good a reason as I've ever heard for changing a Punjabi name," I said, recalling Ahluwalias in India who had abbreviated their name to Walia on the grounds, they joked, of a distaste for *ahlu*—which means people. I pushed on, the American way: "I got your number from my father. I'll be in San Francisco tomorrow. Any chance we might meet?"

Okay, I thought, while I listened to the silence on the line, say no and I'll spare my mother the family's nagging disappointment. Though I would have liked to see the face behind that voice. "How late will you be in town?" he asked. "There are some nice places for a drink."

Great, I thought, another John. "We're not staying the night."

"How are you coming in?" he asked. "I commute from the Peninsula, actually. I'll drop you."

I wanted to tell Mummy I would meet this one alone, but every time I imagined myself drinking in a San Francisco bar with a man I didn't know, regardless of my father's forty-year-old connection, terror seized me. What if Roger turned out to be the serial killer on this list? What if he got drunk and couldn't drive, like John, or worse, pawed me like that American I'd gone out with in college?

Besides, my mother wanted to see San Francisco, and I doubted Uncle Hari would take the time to drive her there. He was still talking about all the time he'd lost driving us to LA Mummy and I took a bus into the city. Buses were too strenuous for my grandmother, so we left her home. We hopped buses, trolleys and cable cars to Chinatown, Ghirardelli Square, Fisherman's Wharf, places I should have visited with Lalita.

Mummy and I met Roger on the corner of Polk and Grant, where he had asked me to look for his white BMW, laughing at my reaction and saying, "Yes, I know. But you really shouldn't judge a person by his car."

The person who stuck his head out the window of the BMW must have been used to being judged by appearances. He was gorgeous: fair skinned, with the prominent cheekbones, jawbones and chin that could make a man's face as striking as a beautiful woman's. His brown hair was long, thick and wavy, swept back over his ears, not a trace of gray, except in his eyes, which glimmered with an ironic humor I had not seen in any of my other dates. I was afraid that I might not find anything wrong with him. I prayed, then feared, that he would reject me for my dark skin and average education as he drove us up and down the hills we'd walked all day, across a relatively flat residential area to a restaurant hanging over the Pacific. All the way he filled my silence with his life story: he had done his undergraduate degree in England; he'd worked for a newspaper in Bradford.

I got interested. "Is that where the Hallowell overtook you?"

He laughed. "It seemed the perfect nom de plume at the time. I'd had to accept Roger practically from birth, which was embarrassing, considering the blokes who still use the name as a verb."

"I don't get it," I said.

"Well, it's eighteenth-century," he said, "roger her and such like."

My face burned. I wondered why men always had to bring up sex. Even American women could not hide their dirty thoughts when they introduced my cousin Kunti with their obscene English pronunciation. I tried to cover up my blushing with a joke. "Is that why you came this side?"

Roger laughed. "I came to New York for a master's in journalism."

"New York?" I said, pressing the conversation on, if only for the sake of my mother, listening to us first in the back seat of Roger's

BMW then across a table at a window overlooking the Pacific on the very edge of America. "*The New York Times.* Time Warner. Why did you ever leave?"

"Friends were going to San Francisco."

"I could live here," I heard myself saying. It was a city, and I wanted to live in the city, not the boring suburbs my uncle had always seemed to favor, not a tourist trap across the border from my mother's promised land. It was on the sea, like Bombay, which Lalita and I had always loved. *Believe me,* she liked to say, *all those tons of falling water are no substitute for salt spray.* She would rather live in Vancouver, she had said so several times, and even if she could not buy a motel there, she could still spend Januaries with me, and in a much more pleasant part of the country than cold, dark Jersey. And when I had a green card I could go to Canada as often as I liked, especially if I didn't have to work from nine to five.

Roger wasn't making millions, but he had a reputation: he had freelanced for every paper in the Bay Area, had been working full-time for one of them for the past five years.

Mummy sat mesmerized by the sunset, or Roger's face, I could not tell which, sipping her Coke. The window looked straight down on a pile of rocks, on which seals were catching the last rays of the sun while the fog crept up to the glowing line of sea and sky. Roger nursed an Irish coffee while I watched him out of the corner of my eye. Could I spend my life, I wondered, with a handsome journalist in San Francisco; would he interfere with the new life I would have to start, support me while I raised our daughter—beautiful, like him, and fair? The heat around my face came back as I wondered if he'd like Lalita. Neither of us would have to tell him she was gay. I was wondering which of us might move from casual conversation to speculation, at least *How long are you staying? When can I see you again?* when Roger said, "Nitasha, there's a path down to the beach. May I show you?"

Great, I thought. Here I thought I'd found the perfect arranged marriage, and he's so anxious to get me alone that he must be the serial rapist I'd avoided with the past four men. I was already shaking my head when my mother said, "Why don't you talk little bit? I want to sit out of the sun."

"You don't have to," I said, but Mummy had already gotten up, picked up her purse and walked across the darkening bar.

I turned from her broad, misshapen back to the last of my mulled wine. "Your mother seems a wise woman," Roger observed. "In fact your family is very much like mine. Well off, conservative. Forgive me if I rush right to it."

"Not at all," I said, forcing myself to look at him to reassure him, reassure myself. I was relieved by the realization that he'd only wanted to talk to me privately. "I like it. I mean, I like to talk."

"Lovely," he said. "Only I'll have to ask—swear you to secrecy, actually—that you never tell anybody what I am about to say. Otherwise we'll have to part. Tonight."

"No," I said, mystified by his clear, honest gray-brown eyes. "I mean, I won't tell anyone."

"You swear? On the head of the person you love most in the world."

Lalita, I thought, without thinking. How Indian of Roger to ask me to swear on someone's head. I saw my mother settle down in a far corner of the bar. "Yes."

He sat back, took a deep breath. "I put off this—looking for a wife—as long as I could. I like the fact that you are older—more mature—past those volatile twenties. Of course we'll have to have children right away."

My heart pounded. Right away? I wanted children, but I did not need a man to tell me when. I was ready to retract my promise, stand up and leave when he said, "Please," touching my hand. My skin contracted beneath his cold palm. "It may be difficult." He did not hold my hand, thank God, but let his fingers slip away across the polished wood as he said, "I will never be the kind of—fully passionate—I mean. Let me put it this way: I have a very good friend; he has been with me for years. To be blunt: anyone I marry will have to—have to accept David."

Without thinking I retorted, "I have a friend," hoping he would respect the same loyalty in a woman. "She spends January with me every year. And I would like to spend some time with her—in the summer."

Roger's face brightened, and the corners of his mouth twitched up. "This is too good to be true." He leaned toward me, across the small, round table. "Then you understand. I am not—can never be—entirely—out. With my family, that is."

"Out," I repeated, the face in front of me shifting back to my last memory of Lalita driving away from the Cleveland airport as I finally realized what Roger had been talking about.

Before I could say anything, he went on, "There is no other way. Is there? I don't think it's necessary—I don't want it to be necessary—to hurt my family. It's one of the reasons we've let them make inquiries, isn't it? That, and the desire for children. It will make them happy. And me. I care very deeply about family. It's just that—well, after many years—some of them hell, as you may well know—I understand myself, and I don't want to live any more lies than I have to." I couldn't find my voice. "Oh. In case you're wondering. I have discussed my plans with David. He happens to be married himself. His children mean very much to him."

I would have given anything for Lalita to be sitting there beside me. How her laughter would have pulled me back from the tears that clouded my vision. I whisked a cocktail napkin to my face. "Needless to say," Roger went on, "you may tell your friend."

I found my voice: "My friend is just a friend."

"Oh," he said, a frown creasing the skin around his gray-brown eyes. "I've upset you. I'm sorry."

It took all of my will to hide my tears from my mother, who was sitting across the bar staring at us, trying to figure out, I knew, how my conversation with Roger was progressing.

"All I can do is give you time," he said. The sun had set, and the window table suddenly felt cold. "I'm willing to correspond, call, visit, as you like."

I would not have told Mummy even if I'd had the chance. I couldn't. I was sworn. Lalita would have laughed at my fear of hexing her, but would have kept Roger's confidence for reasons of her own. Of course my mother insisted that Roger come in and have dinner with my aunt and uncle, my grandmother. She had to, after he had bought our drinks and driven us all the way down the Peninsula. It would have been equally impolite for him to refuse. We sat with my uncle, aunt and grandmother. Even Rosa came home before Roger left. And then I had to listen to my mother's, grandmother's, aunt's, cousin's, even Hari Uncle's praise. "Such a nice boy," my mother said; "A good family boy," my grandmother agreed; "So good looking," my aunt added; "Well off too," said Hari Uncle. "He is *hot*," Rosa said. "Why was he not snatched up twenty years ago?"

I could have told them, Roger *had* been snatched up. But they would have accused me of making up a nasty rumor to get out of this one, and, besides, Lalita's head hung in the balance.

In the morning I said goodbye to my mother at the door of Hari Uncle's house. Auntie Jill was going to drop me at the airport then drive straight to Hari Uncle's garage. Mummy begged me to stay for a few more days and see Roger Hallowell again. My grandmother insisted that I marry him as soon as an astrologer could name a date— she did not expect to live much longer, Kunti could never have a proper marriage, the other cousins were not old enough, and she wanted to see a grandchild's wedding before she died. "I hope you realize," Jill said, as she drove up the arrivals ramp, "that your uncle and I will support you, whatever decision you make."

I wish I could have believed that, even though I realized she was not talking financially. For the entire flight I practiced how I would tell Lalita, when. Could I wait until she came to visit me in January? Could I tell her such a story over the telephone? I could not bear the thought of telling her without being able to see her reaction. My mother would be flying back to Jersey after Christmas, and she was bringing my grandmother for three or four weeks before they would travel to India together. I closed my eyes and saw the four of us, stretched across the beige wall-to-wall of my one-room apartment, none of us asleep.

My nerves rose close to the skin and stayed there, all the way across the country to which Mummy and Daddy had sent me, not having the slightest idea how lonely an American life could be. Even if they came, I would have no one who really understood me, and if they died, I would be without anyone for the rest of my life. When the plane landed I used the cash my mother had shoved into my hand to buy a ticket to Niagara Falls. Halfway across New York I thought better of running to Lalita and considered catching the next plane back, if there was one. But as soon as I got off the plane I found a telephone and called her. One good thing about the motel business, someone always picks up the phone.

Her Toyota pulled up before rush hour was over. "What?" she said, hoisting my oversized duffle into the trunk. "What?"

I asked her, even before she had driven out of the airport, "Would you marry a gay man?"

"No," she said. "I wouldn't marry a man at all. Why? Don't tell me they found you a gay?"

She was too smart. Laughing she asked, "Why has he said yes to an arranged marriage, the hypocrite?"

"Children," I said. "He cares a great deal for family."

"Enough to tell one lies."

"Have you told your family?"

With a deep sigh she said, "I told them as much as they would let me: that I did not want them wasting time and embarrassing themselves looking for a husband, would not meet men for any purpose, including marriage, that I was not dating anyone, had never dated anyone, and would never fall in love with any man."

I wished I could have said the same. "Did it stop them from fixing you up?"

She nodded. "They think I'm pure. A cross between the nuns in our convent school and the goddess Saraswati, who had more on her mind than procreation."

"Wisdom," I tried to remember, wishing I had enough to figure out how I was going to procreate without at least sleeping with a man.

"For a long time I was." She smirked. "Pure, I mean. Of course, you know that. You, of all people. And then there was this woman. One of my professors."

"A professor," I said. "La!"

"That does not mean anything," she said, as she negotiated Route 62 with the expertise of an independent woman. "Not now. Not for a long time. It never did. This Roger Hallowell. Has he made you an offer?"

I nodded, my stomach tight and my heart absolutely paining. "Anyone he marries will have to accept his friend."

She laughed. "He said that? Why doesn't he live with his friend? Or does he?"

"The friend is married. Was your professor married?"

"A modern, American joint family," she said, ignoring my question. "Right in your line."

"Are you saying I should do it?"

"If you want to keep the secret."

"I can't pretend to be a normal American—Indian—wife while he's with—and he wants—how will we have children?"

"Turkey baster."

"La!"

"He'll be able to get you pregnant, 'Tash. Gay doesn't mean you can't screw a girl and think of a guy—or vice versa."

"Lalita!"

"If you can *get* pregnant. Between the two of us you've got a better chance of having at least one baby. Did you ever think of that?"

"Lala, you're outrageous." I didn't know whether to laugh or cry.

"A real shame girls can't get married. You could marry him, get your green card, then get a divorce and marry me. I would move to California without even thinking about it. Maybe I can buy a hotel there. I'll look into it. This guy, certainly, will not mind if I came out and spent a proper rest of our lives with you."

She was right. He'd as much as said so. I tried to imagine Lalita wrapped up in bright silks neither of us ever wore, greeting Roger's David with a marigold garland at the traditional arrival of the boy's family. Would she sing the songs to me that ladies always sang the night before the wedding, shameless, ribald songs about the new wife's duties? Would she stay with me when it was over, after Roger had gone to a hotel with David?

"For years you would not come to see my tacky motel," she said as we approached a line of braking cars, their tail lights glowing, at a row of booths, like toll booths, at the border. "For fear that your ex-pired visa would not get you back into the land of opportunity. Has that changed?"

"I'm not sure I want to go back."

"You say that now. Will you say it six months from now?"

"Six months from now it will be summer, even in Canada."

"Mr. Right can always sponsor you for immigration," she said, "if he wants you that much."

"Mr. Right doesn't exactly want *me*."

"All you need for permanent residence in Canada is money," she said. "I have that."

The red lights of Hondas, Toyotas, Fords cleared for a moment as a tear made its way out of my eye.

"I think I can manage the family without much trouble," Lalita went on. "And I'll help you with yours. They're our parents, 'Tash, and they will love us no matter what we tell them. If it's too difficult for your family, I'll have the babies."

"No, I want a baby," I said, my voice breaking as the sobs came out.

"Wait," she said, putting her hand on my thigh as I pressed my arms across my chest, trying to keep in what I did not want to cry. "We don't want the border patrol to think I'm taking an illegal alien across the border for illicit purposes."

A fair-haired man in a uniform asked to see my passport. I hadn't brought it. Even if my uncle or the LA cousins had been willing to drive us all the way to Mexico, I would not have gone. I'd heard too many horror stories about Indians being taken for illegal Hispanics at the border. I passed the customs official my driver's license. Though I could never afford a car, my uncle Hari had taught me how to drive.

"Can I see your green card?" the official asked, peering across La-lita into the car as he returned my license.

"She's a U. S. citizen," Lalita said. "Besides, what does Canada have to do with a U. S. green card?"

"Without a passport or green card, I can't let you in."

"But she was born in New York," Lalita lied.

"You'll have to drive back and get her passport," he said.

"I'm just miles from my own motel," she said. "Niagara Nivas. Do you know it?"

"I'm sorry. You can turn around right ahead, just after the cone. The car there will accompany you."

A Canadian patrol car sat just fifty feet in front of us, in case Lalita tried to rush the border. I put my hand on her hand, on the wheel. "Let's turn around," I said. "I may be able to catch a night flight."

"I'm not letting you fly home," she said, *her* eyes watery.

"Don't do anything stupid," I whispered. "Even Roger can't bring me back from India."

She took the U-turn and drove us back along the highway. I felt anger well up in my chest. Thirteen years in the United States and to be recognized as an American I'd have to marry someone I did not love. "I don't belong anywhere," I blurted out. "I may as well go back to India."

"We don't belong in India," Lalita said, glaring at the road, the neon lights of motels and restaurants piercing the early dark. "They marry the girl to the mother-in-law, not the boy. Which may not be bad, depending on the mother-in-law." When I didn't respond to her stupid joke, she went on: "No. Really. Separation of the sexes has some real advantages. But no one lives in a joint family anymore. You belong with me. You always have. When I get back I'll mail you the immigration papers."

She turned the wheel and stopped the car in the parking lot of a long motel outlined with a row of bright, white lights. The desk clerk, a bald, plump Indian, who could have been Lalita's uncle, gave us a room with two double beds, a bright, white bathroom that hummed when the light was on, and a view of the highway, a long, loud river of cars running parallel to the strip of ugly rooms. Lalita laughed and

flopped onto a bed. I stretched out on the other one. "This is ridiculous," I said, staring at the textured ceiling. I felt the mattress shift as
Lalita crawled onto the bed beside me.

"We'll go out and have some dinner," she said, "decide what to
do in the morning."

I felt her take my hair in both hands and smooth it, the way she
used to when she used to braid it for me, when we had been kids.
"I've got to call Mummy," I said, "pretend that I got in all right, so
she won't call the apartment and wonder where I am."

"You're right where you belong," she insisted, moving from my
hair to my back, after all day on two planes, a massage I desperately
needed. But the more she touched me, the more my heart filled; I
was afraid it might burst, flooding my body and floating me over the
falls with its warm, rich blood. This time I turned to her, not to tickle
her soft sides but to draw her heavy body down on mine. Pulling her
curly hair around my face, I breathed the perfume of her sweet
shampoo. And I was still afraid, still in double mind, even as I felt her
smooth full lips on mine, as her hands caressed the skin beneath my
sweater, pushed my jeans onto the floor and drew both sides of me
together, if only for an instant, only for a time.

10 First Generation

Shawn, Sheela, Nitasha, Shakuntala, Ranjit
New Brunswick, New Jersey

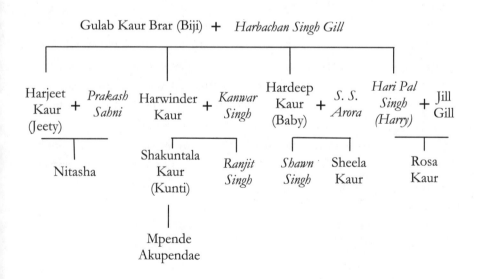

1

Shawn Singh Arora

RANJIT DID NOT look good. The circles under his eyes were darker than any I had ever seen, even after a week of all-nighters. I had one semester left at Harvard when he was only starting at Rutgers, though he was born two months before me, twenty-one years ago. And it was no advantage he could legally go out and buy liquor for his fellow freshmen. Living on the road in Africa and Europe, drinking, and whatever else he had been doing for the past four years had turned his skin absolutely yellow. His T-shirt and jeans reeked of smoke—tobacco and marijuana—and his breath smelled like the stench that filled the fraternity after my brothers and I had been binging our stress away all weekend with grain alcohol and beer.

I backed out of a hug in the doorway of his sister, Kunti's one-bedroom apartment, in a hideous New Jersey town under the false name of *New* Brunswick. I would not have known Ranjit was in the country if my mother had not called to tell me he had passed through London. He was, in her exact words, "Bad. And you know my sister has no money. But how am I to refuse a kid in the family? And he frightened me!"

"How much did you give him?" I asked. "If you give anybody anything it should be me. With Sheela crashing with me on her way home from California, everything costs double."

I had a job lined up on Wall Street, but I couldn't get an advance on my salary, and my sister, that was Sheela, was a miser with the money she had saved working in a Chinese restaurant in the San Fernando Valley. "This money is for college," she whined. "In India because I can't afford the Ivy League like you."

"Why does a girl have to go to an Ivy League college?" I asked. "You don't even want to stay in this country."

"That's not the point. I deserve as much as you. I'm your sister."

"Fine. We'll divide the money. You'll still have enough to live in India. It's cheaper there."

"It's only cheaper for spoiled brats like you!"

Spoiled brat? I couldn't even afford a car. It took me two weeks to borrow one to drive me and my sister to New Jersey. I hadn't seen Ranjit since he had put me on a train in Rome. Our motorcycle tour of Europe was our last bash before my mum and dad sent Sheela and me to our aunt's house in California. But the tour went sour even before Ranjit and I left London. We're lucky the husband of the girl he picked up didn't find and kill all three of us. We got as far as Rome before we abandoned plans to cycle all the way to Africa. I went back to England, glad to see the last of my cousin. And when I was a kid I used to beg my mother to send me to his house in Nairobi.

I'd tasted my first beer with him, smoked my first cigarette, after trying marijuana. I watched him lay that girl he'd picked up in London, and I had plenty myself in front of him. A regular orgy on that Europe trip. He hasn't been the same since she dropped him. I called Nairobi to try to talk him into coming to Massachusetts. If he needed to finish high school, he could go for free in Cambridge. He might not get into Harvard, but there were a pile of colleges in Boston. "What do I need with college?" he said.

"Credentials. You'll get a job here, and, besides, it's fun. What are you doing, otherwise?"

"I'm taking a trip to Europe."

"We did that!"

"Through Ethiopia this time."

"You can't cross the desert on a bike!"

He spent a long time in Europe, according to my Mum, and would have stayed if he hadn't gotten sick.

I sat down in the middle of Kunti's living room, on the worn, green wall-to-wall between Ranjit and his sister, propped against the wall next to the door, and Asante, Kunti's baby's father, sitting on a folded-up sleeping bag, army green, against the far wall between two old-fashioned sash windows. What was he doing home, I wondered. Ranjit said Asante stayed with the baby every day then went out after Kunti came home from the laboratory, where she washed test tubes or something. She hardly saw him anymore, which would have made the family happy if he'd either marry her or move out. He beat up Kunti's father, I had heard, my uncle Kanwar, when Uncle Kanwar came all the way from Africa to force Kunti to have an abortion. But then everybody beat up Uncle Kanwar. Aunt Harwinder told my mother that she must have slapped him for every time he pummeled her, and she bragged that Ranjit beat his father "like a true Sardar!" As if all Sikhs are good for is combat. I swear sometimes I think the family perpetuates these stereotypes better than the narrow-minded Brits I grew up with.

Sheela sank into a broken down cushion on the couch next to Nitasha, the eldest of us cousins, the most authentic, from the source, I called her, India, a traditional joint family—an experience that would give *me* sexual dysfunction, and I have always considered my cousin Nitasha seriously sexually retarded. Thirty-one, and she was still not married. For a guy that's fine, as long as he can get a girl every time he needs one. But for a girl it's not quite decent—not to mention pushing the biological clock. I had never seen Nitasha with a guy. Even with the network of our aunts and uncles all over the world, she could not find a husband. Her best friend, Lalita Das, was sitting on the floor leaning against the couch, her big hair brushing up against 'Tash's knee. "In from Canada for the Fahrenheit temperatures?" I asked.

Lalita smirked. I swear that girl was not a woman. She had shoulders like a football player gone to fat. Nitasha was what they call the femme in this relationship, not bad looking—she's our mother's sister's kid, after all—petite with large, full breasts, straight, long, glossy hair, the kind you want to grab with both hands. What a waste of female flesh. First time I remember her she was flying kites with her cousins on her father's side, all older than us, from the flat roof of her house in Bombay. Even then this girl was always with her.

Ranjit ripped open a six-pack sitting on the floor and lobbed me a beer. Thank God I caught it. Otherwise Kunti's kid, running around the room in a frenzied attempt to keep herself awake, would have suffered her first head injury, as far as I could tell by the smoothness of her polished skull. Hindus shave the head at about a year or so, but neither Kunti nor Asante were Hindu, for one thing, and the kid was a lot older than a year. She was running, for god sakes, babbling, "Gimme, gimme, gimme." Why they'd shaved her head, like her father's, was beyond me. Girls should be girls.

Ranjit held a can up to my sister. She shook her head, the poster child, as she always was, even in California, for sobriety and abstinence. Kunti grabbed the can out of her brother's hand and popped the tab like the expert she was at twenty-six. I held my can up to Nitasha. "No, thank you," she said. "We don't drink beer."

Ranjit pushed himself off the floor. "Give me some money, Shawn. What'll you have? Wine? Whiskey?"

"I don't have any money," I said.

"Don't go out in that cold," Nitasha said. "Don't you remember when we all came here for Hari Uncle's wedding? You started crying as soon as we got outside the International Arrivals building: 'I don't like this America.'"

"You remember that trip?" Kunti asked.

"I was just a few months old," Sheela said.

"Shawn, how old were we?" Ranjit asked. "Three? Must have left a mark. *Still* don't like the place. But necessity is necessity. C'mon. Let's buy these girls a drink."

"I'm not going out," I said. "It's fifteen degrees. I told you, I don't have any money."

The kid started to whine. "Oh, Mpende, Mpende," Nitasha said, dangling a scruffy stuffed lion in front of the kid's bleary eyes.

Sheela asked, "What did you call her?"

"It's Swahili," Kunti said. "It means 'You are loved.'"

"Mpende." Sheela looked across the room at the baby's father, scowling since we'd all come in, and said, "I don't know your last name."

Oh, Sheela, Sheela, I thought. Even Asante was not his name. He had changed it, Kunti told me, in a fit of nationalism for a continent he had never seen, though in Kunti he had the best of both worlds—an African who wasn't even black. Judging from Asante's tint—a shade darker than my natural tan, a few shades lighter than Lalita's—only a fraction of his ancestors could have come from Africa. But I'd been in this country long enough to know: Americans only perceive two colors, white and black. Even third-generation Asians get asked, "Where you from?" As if they could just go back and take up where their great-grandparents left off, before World War II, Communism, Korea or Vietnam.

"We gave Mpende her own last name," Asante grunted.

"Akupendae," Kunti said.

"You are loved," Ranjit translated, with more than a little sarcasm, I thought, "by the one who is loved by you."

"How romantic," Sheela said.

Lalita broke into a smile, but I doubt even she and Nitasha had ever experienced the synergy embodied in that love child's name. I know I hadn't. Ranjit *wished* he had with that woman in Europe, but she was only using him to get away from her husband. In this company I felt a wave of relief that in two-three weeks I would take my baby sister to the airport. In India, everyone in the family agreed, a girl was far less likely to get pregnant by an African-American and want to keep the baby, or, alternatively, to give up men entirely and fall in love with a woman.

2

Sheela Kaur Arora

It was the first time I had seen any of my cousins except Uncle Hari's daughter, Rosa, since Mum had sent me and Shawn to California five years ago. Everyone had changed. Ranjit was weak, as my mother said. *His* mother thought America would cure him. I don't know where anyone in my family got their ideas. Maybe if he spent his tuition money on detoxification and joined a twelve-step program instead of a fraternity like my brother. I watched Ranjit light a cigarette and pass it to Kunti. Smoking had etched lines beside her mouth. She had dyed her long, straight hair a brassy red that made her fair face look unnaturally dark. She was still pretty; she had always been the prettiest of all of us—except Rosa, who had the tall, slim body of an American model, the best of Indian and European features on her unforgettable face. On Kunti's face a hardness had developed, as if, like her mother, my aunt Harwinder, she was always thinking about something that caused her excruciating pain. Her daughter, Mpende Akupendae, running from Nitasha to the wall across the room, from the wall to me, me to the wall, wall to Nitasha, incessantly, was beautiful, with big brown eyes and creamy skin. I had not expected the baby to be fair. At the time that Kunti's mother called and told my mother that Kunti was pregnant, my mother had made a fuss about the father being black. My father is the tolerant member of the family; besides, Mum rarely disagrees with her sisters. But the guy sitting underneath the window was no darker than Nitasha or her friend Lalita. His features were not particularly African either—his nose was long and sharp, his lips thin. I couldn't say about his hair—or Mpende's, for that matter. Their heads were as smooth as river stones, about the same color.

I was fed up with the attitude toward color in this country, not that London or the family or both hadn't given me an attitude of my own. Californians were either Mexican, Asian or White, according to the unofficial "peoples'" census, with whites claiming Spanish place names as if they had ordered them direct from Madrid. Delivery people, white and black, took me for the maid of the white, Jewish family I lived with in Los Angeles, those clever enough to have retained their high school Spanish sometimes addressing me, "*Hola, Señorita!*" How polite they could be when I had the energy to assert my identity: "Indian? No kidding? *Om, Shanti*. Let it be."

In England, in some ways, things had been even worse. The British were more familiar with India, having owned it. But they hated us even more for not staying in our place. But what was our place? Only Nitasha had been raised in India; none of us had any control over where we were brought up. But I could go anywhere I pleased. This country had given me that versatility. Just three-four months in England, and I would show my parents acceptance to a university they could afford with English currency. Imagine it: with my British passport and American green card, a foreign student in the country of my mother's childhood! (I can't say birth; she was born in what is now Pakistan.)

Ranjit, standing by the door trying to get my brother to go with him to buy some liquor, worked his hand into the pocket of his jeans and eased out a plastic bag full of dried brown leaves I recognized as marijuana. "No way," I said.

I'd been known to leave a party when someone broke out the pot. Squeamishness, I guess. I can't stand the smell, don't like the stupid way druggies act, and can't see the point of breaking the law to alter one's state of consciousness anyway. But Shawn and I had nowhere else to sleep. Shawn knew that I was fundamentally opposed to drugs—they were just too common in the high school we had gone to in California—but Shawn was a Greek-lettered party animal, and marijuana didn't bother him. It didn't even bother him, from what I could tell, that Ranjit's mother had sent him here specifically to detoxify. There were no drunk tanks in Nairobi, she had told my mother, and she did not want to send him to India, where only my aunt Jeety, Nitasha's mother, lived anymore, or England, to my mother, because the last time he was in England he had gotten involved with a married woman. My African cousins were fast, no question about it. I'd seen a lot of self-destructive men and women like Ranjit and Kunti in Los Angeles, and frankly I was tired of all the self-indulgence, the way this country makes promiscuity, drinking, even the illegal pleasures easier to get than a college degree. I was looking for the words to ask Ranjit not to smoke when Asante beat me to it: "You know I don't allow no drugs in here."

Kunti laughed. Asante glared at her. "When you pay the rent," she said, "you can tell my family what to do in my apartment. Meanwhile I'd like to get high."

"In front of Mpende?" Nitasha said.

"What do you want me to do?" Kunti said. "Put her out?"

Before I knew what was happening, Asante leapt up, strode across the room, scooped Mpende out of Nitasha's lap, and carried her into the bedroom. Mpende let out a scream. "Hey," Kunti said, pushing herself off the floor. "Where are you going?"

"Out."

"Not with her."

Nitasha followed Kunti into the bedroom. "I'll watch her," she said.

I heard Kunti say, "She hates that snowsuit."

Asante answered, "You want your daughter to freeze?"

"Asante?" Nitasha went on. "You go ahead. She'll be all right. I'll stay with her in this room. I don't smoke. You know that."

"I know," he said, "that you would be the first to change the lock as soon as I walk out."

Lalita got up and walked silently into the bedroom.

"It's Kunti's apartment," Nitasha said. "If she wants to change anything, she can go right ahead and do it."

"Go back to the living room, Nitasha," Kunti said. "I'll handle this."

3

Nitasha Sahni

Why was Asante so upset? I'd done him a favor by moving out, and that was years ago, before Mpende had been born. He and I had more in common than he thought, at least as far as drugs were concerned. I didn't mind a glass of wine every now and then. I have even tried smoking—with Lalita, in India, when we were in our teens, but I don't like the habit, and Lalita has always wanted to make me happy, so she quit. We tried marijuana, *bhang* in India, but I felt completely out of control—I smiled when I didn't want to, laughed when nothing was funny. I hate that.

I went back into the living room and asked Ranjit to put the marijuana away. As the oldest, and he was nine years younger than me, I had a duty to protect my cousins. "You shouldn't smoke in front of your niece," I said. "You shouldn't even drink."

He laughed. "My father was giving me scotch from the time I turned thirteen."

"No way," Sheela said.

"He said it would make me a man."

"Hah!" Shawn said.

"You think I'm not a man?"

He clenched his fists and presented Shawn his left shoulder. He looked pathetic, thin and sallow. Shawn laughed. I was wondering what to say to prevent Ranjit from hitting Shawn when Kunti came out of the bedroom with her coat on. "Let's go," she said. "He'll watch her."

I looked at Lalita. We couldn't stay. We were exhausted. We had been packing for three days, arguing for two weeks before that. For that reason Lalita had not had the time to drive me to New Brunswick to see Ranjit, though my mother kept calling to urge me to go and talk him into "getting treatment for this *alcoolism*." That Lalita was still arguing with me, still in Jersey City showed, I guess, how much she cared. She just would not give up on me, and I could not give her up either.

I had gotten calls for months after my mother had come to visit me. One or two of the "boys" she had introduced me to wanted to see me again. But I couldn't imagine being married to any one of them, even my father's friend's son, Roger. Though I think I understood him best. I just didn't want to live the lie of family life with a husband who would rather be with his married male lover. At the same time I could never be the conventional wife my mother was.

If I wanted to be sure I would be able to stay on this continent, to visit India anytime I had the money, go back and forth across the American border, as Lalita could, whenever she had the time off to see me, I would have to go back to Niagara Falls and accept the immigration Lalita had obtained for me in Canada. I could give up my dead-end job assigning beds in a New York hospital, live rent free in Lalita's motel, and with the one person in the world I knew I could spend the rest of my life with. There was no down side, Lalita had convinced me, except the six months of cold, my mother's disappointment, and the chance that some of our acquaintances, family and friends might come to the conclusion that Lalita and I were closer than the average friends. And whose business was that? I did not feel enlightened by the knowledge that Kunti and Asante were no longer having sex. Or so she was always telling me when I came to play with Mpende. I didn't care that Ranjit had kept a woman in the house next door to his in Nairobi, that she had run off with the boy who had taken Kunti's virginity, though I thought the whole thing a stupid reason for embarking on a self-destructive, slow suicidal, alcoholic binge. I didn't care who Shawn was sleeping with, that Sheela was still a virgin, or anything else about my cousins' love lives. So why should they care about mine?

Lalita and I put on our jackets with the others, but when we got outside in the cold, dark street, I said, "Okay. See you. I'll give you a call tomorrow."

Lalita walked to her Toyota, pulled up to the crumbling curb, and opened the door for me.

"Why?" Kunti said. "We're just going to get something to eat. Aren't you hungry?"

"You can get that drink Shawn wouldn't buy you," Ranjit said.

"I told you," Shawn said. "I don't have any money. Where's all the money you brought from England?"

"I didn't bring any money."

I had the urge to put my arm around Lalita's waist, so separate did I feel from my mother's sisters' kids, but I would not have done that in this group, had only done it in public at all *before* Lalita had told me how she felt, and besides, she had walked around to the other side of the car.

"We just got here," Sheela said. "Can we come to your place later?"

"Are you still at the same place?" Shawn asked.

I guess I should have told them all—upstairs, before the wind cut through my clothes like freezing fire, forcing me to stamp my feet and shiver. But they would tell their mothers, their mothers would get on the phone with my mother. "Please don't tell anyone," I said. "I haven't told Mummy. I'm giving up my apartment, leaving tomorrow for Canada." I could just feel Lalita smiling.

"It's cold enough here!" Shawn said.

"Let's get out of this shit," Ranjit said. "We can talk in the bar."

"I'm not twenty-one," Sheela said.

I got into the car beside Lalita. "Let's go home," I said. "I'd better call India. One of them is sure to tell her. If Shawn and Sheela want to stay with us, Shawn knows where I live."

She pulled into the lane beside the row of parked cars, shimmering in the cold artificial light of the American street. "I don't feel close to them," I said. "I never did. I feel closer to my cousins on my father's side."

"Well, you all grew up in different countries," Lalita said.

"Our mothers never thought that was an obstacle," I said. "But you know. It was hell living with Kunti."

4

Shakuntala Kaur

I climbed into the back seat of the Volvo Shawn had driven down from Massachusetts. "Shawn," I said. "A Wolliwo?"

Ranjit and I had always made fun of the way my mother and father confused their w's and v's.

"Relax," Shawn said. "It's not mine."

I nudged my brother, slouched beside me in the back, and pointed to the bag bulging in the pocket of his jeans, then brought my fingers up to my lips and made smoke-sucking noises. He pulled out the weed and a pack of papers.

"'Tasha's not waiting for us," Sheela said, peering through the windshield from the front seat next to Shawn.

"She's got a hot date tonight," I said. My brother laughed.

"Really?" Sheela said. "Mum's looking for a boy for her."

"Oh, everybody's looking for a boy for 'Tasha," I said. "They've been looking for a boy for her ever since I came."

"Don't be dense," her brother said, pulling into the deserted, dark street I could not afford to move away from.

Ranjit's hands shook as he rolled the paper around the loose grass.

"Are you sick again?" I asked. He'd had this stomach pain on and off since he had come from Nairobi. Mum said he had problems with his liver. She wanted me to check him into a hospital, but how was I to pay for hospitalization on my salary? Ranjit had no insurance. She accused me of denying my brother medical attention because of something as insignificant as money. I told her I hadn't had anything much more significant than plain bread and rice since Mpende had been born. She said to ask Nitasha to get me a special price at the hospital where she had no power even to take a day off when she wanted to.

"Unsmooth ride for a Swedish car," Ranjit mumbled.

"Where to?" Shawn asked.

"Oh, just drive," I said. "If Asante weren't such a hypocrite we wouldn't have to do this in a car."

"Do what?" Sheela asked.

"Sheela," I said, "you really are naïve."

Ranjit took a hit and passed the joint to me. I inhaled as much as I could—believe me, I needed it! Then I bypassed the nineteen-year-old just saying no in the front seat and stretched over the back of the seat to hand it to Shawn. "While you're driving?" Sheela said. "We don't even know where we are."

"Turn here," I said. "I know where I am."

"Anybody got any money?" Ranjit asked.

Shawn said, "I thought *you* had money."

"Where would I get money?"

"Don't remind me," I said, exhaling. He'd already gone through everything I'd had for the month, and he'd only been here for two weeks. That's why I was so mad at Asante. If he didn't pay the rent, no one would.

"My mother gave you some," Shawn said.

"She did?" I said. Ranjit hadn't told me.

"That was just for London," he said.

"You shouldn't be driving," Sheela said.

Shawn glanced at Sheela. "*You* have money."

"Not with me," Sheela answered.

"How do you expect me to buy gas?"

"Your girlfriend filled it up before we left."

"Girlfriend!" Ranjit said.

They went on, but I didn't hear a word. I got to thinking about Mpende, Asante back there in the apartment. Sometimes when I came home from the lab, he and Mpende weren't there. I felt my arms begin to tingle at the very memory of the first time he failed to bring her home. It was dark. It was twenty degrees. He could not have taken her for a walk, and where would they drive to? I called all of the emergency rooms. I called the restaurant where Asante used to work. I called the one friend of his whose number I knew, the bouncer at a bar Asante once worked in. No one knew where he was. I panicked. I could almost feel the panic in Shawn's girlfriend's car, cruising aimlessly through the dark streets I'd walked that night. And it was not a safe neighborhood—dealers on the corners, homeless men and women asking for money, pickpockets, muggers. Everybody called Mpende an unwanted child, unplanned, but I had wanted her; Nitasha once said she thought I had planned to get pregnant so that I could show my parents, in her warped opinion, how wrong they were about my chances of achieving the American dream by becoming the rich, American doctor they wanted. I told her I was only following her lead on that one. When I had walked back into the apartment that night, tears frozen to my lashes, I saw Asante, still in his coat and knit cap, pacing the room, Mpende curled up on the couch, taking those deep breaths that always reassured me.

"Where the hell were you?" he shouted. "I'm supposed to work at eight o'clock! I can't leave her here alone."

"Where were you? I've been out looking for you since five-thirty!"

"I can't talk to you. I've got to go."

To teach him a lesson, I packed my nightgown and a change of clothes, bundled Mpende up, and took the train to Jersey City. It was always a pain carrying Mpende on the trains. I wished my mother had bought me a car when she had come to see Mpende. But she hadn't brought enough money for a car, and Uncle Hari would not buy her one, even though he had just bought his own car-repair franchise in California. "How will you ever afford insurance?" he asked. "You're complaining now you can't afford food." From the subway, because of my cheap uncle, I had to carry Mpende through that cold to Nitasha's apartment building then wait while she answered the doorbell.

"What happened?" she asked.

I told her Asante had hit me. I was crying so hard. Nitasha said a few choice things about him, about men in general and asked me what I'd ever seen in him. I told her I couldn't stand him anymore, the way he kept quitting jobs because the boss, if he was white, was *the man*; if he was black, an uncle Tom. While I kept working in the lab because I didn't know what else to do. It didn't matter to Asante if he didn't work. He let me pay the rent, buy food—and then he ate it, leaving me with nothing.

At about three in the morning Nitasha's phone rang. "Don't pick it up," I said, still awake on the adrenaline it took to run away with Mpende in the night. "I'm trying to show him who has control of this baby."

"It could be Mummy," she said, her voice all slow with sleep. "She always calls me in the middle of the night."

She picked it up, and when she said, "No, she isn't here," I almost gave myself away by laughing. She hung up. She told me he did not believe her, and he had threatened, if I ever "pulled that stunt again," to take Mpende and never bring her back.

But he didn't disbelieve her enough to come out after us in his car in the middle of the night. I woke *him* up in the morning. I had to leave Mpende with somebody, and Nitasha would not take the day off to watch her. I *couldn't* take off. I needed the money. "How do you intend to get a judge to grant you custody?" I shouted. "You may be the father but you're not my husband. You can't hold a job. You can't even stay in school—"

"When did I ever have the money to pay a university to teach me the crap the white man taught you? You used to listen when I told you how it is. And if I got to work, how do I get the time to go to school? You rich bitch. You run out of money and you call your mother, your rich aunt in London, your uncle, the Midas muffler man in California! Who am I gonna call?"

"That's no reason to live off of me. I don't have anything. All three of them, this whole family says I've got to make it on my own. And even you won't help!"

Then my brother moved in and wouldn't help either. He was supposed to start the spring semester at Rutgers, but neither one of us had the money to pay his tuition. Mum hadn't sent anything with him, or so he said. She had not been working since St. Francis' Academy for Girls had dismissed her, and my father not only did not pay the bills, he was not even living at home anymore. The last time I had seen him, at my uncle Hari's three years ago, he had said he would tell all of our friends in Nairobi I got married, though Asante refused to see him, let alone apologize for wrestling him to the floor when he showed up at the door of my apartment. And neither of us wanted to get married. Girls had babies all the time in America; there was no reason to get married. Asante said that. I believed him. And now I needed someone to sponsor me for permanent residence in the United States, and I couldn't stand him enough to marry him.

"I wonder what that jerk is doing with Mpende," I asked my brother, my cousins in the car. "Let's get take-out and go back."

"Let's not," Shawn said, and to his sister, "You've got to have at least one traveler's check."

"Drop me off at the apartment," I said. "You can find food on your own. Bring me a hamburger or something."

"The kid'll be okay," Ranjit said.

"You don't know," I said. "He said he'd take her where I'd never find her."

"Shit, I think my sister's got the paranoia," Ranjit said.

"I'd say so," said Shawn.

"What?" I said. "What are you saying about me? Drive me back. If not I'll walk."

"You can't walk in this neighborhood," Sheela said.

I bothered them until they dropped me at the door, and I made Ranjit come up with me, just in case Asante wasn't there, in case he'd taken her and we would have to go out looking for his car to get her back. If he tried to raise my daughter in his car, I'd get the police to arrest him. What did I care if they deported me? Mpende was *my* child of *my* body. I would deny that I had ever had sex with Asante, someone else was the father, in Africa. What did Americans want with another mixed-race child anyway? They would fly us home, where I would not have to worry about who I left her with when I went out. We had guards, a driver, the houseboy and the cook, my mother's maid and their families. I could hire one of their daughters as a nanny. And without my father in the house, without Ranjit, it would be just me and my mother, and she had gotten a lot easier to get along with when she realized that just like Ranjit I wasn't going to do what she wanted.

5

Ranjit Singh

My sister can't hold her smoke. She dragged me up three flights out of paranoia. And the kid was there. On the divan, the way I liked her best—unconscious. Asante sat up in his sleeping bag.

"You can go," Kunti said, dropping her coat on the arm of the divan.

"You thought I was going to take her," Asante said.

I left them to fight it out. Grass is mellow, but not mellow enough. Beer's just piss. I told Shawn I'd meet him at a pizza restaurant on Hamilton. He could leave me a slice, I didn't care.

"It's cold," he said. "You're not used to it."

I wouldn't feel the cold if I could just get fifteen, twenty minutes away from the cousins. Shawn was great. For five-ten minutes. On our Europe trip, he got all bent about my girl. Then he came to this cold place. I got one or two phone calls after he had been in California for a year: "'Jit!" He never called me that. It was American. "They say you've got a liver problem. Is that true?"

"Bullshit," I told him. "What I've got is family problems."

"Me too. All I have to do is get a cold. Mum gives my aunt hell for not checking me into the nearest hospital, and I'm not even living there—I moved out. One of my friends, a Jewish guy . . . Are you drinking? I mean a beer or two's all right, even a Saturday night drunk, know what I mean? But every day can be a problem."

"Shawn, I've been drinking a whole a lot longer than you," I said. "And believe me, there's a lot more out there besides beer and whiskey."

On my last trip I made friends without his interference. Some with motorcycles. It was family. Better than any family I'd ever had. I got sick, or I'd still be in Amsterdam, with my friends.

Shawn's girlfriend's Volvo cruised at five kilometers or so next to me as I walked. I could hear Shawn laughing, see him leaning over Sheela to shout out the open window next to her, "Ranjit, you half-witted Sardar!"

So I was a half-wit. Like my father. My mother always said so. I slipped between two old brick apartment buildings, like Kunti's. The guy I wanted was usually somewhere in the neighborhood. I just had to hang around. He'd come out: *what do you need?*

I'd have to ask for credit. He'd give it to me. He got all the cash I brought. Junkies, as we called ourselves in Europe, are honest, sharing people. If one of us had something, all of us got a little, even if it only took the edge off. Even the dealers cut us breaks.

I walked around the block three times, making sure the Volvo had moved on. It was only Shawn and Sheela now. They could drive straight back to Massachusetts for all I cared. I wished I'd gotten some money out of them.

No sign of my dealer. The cold cut through my jacket. Why my sister stayed here when she could be slouching in our garden in Nairobi I will never understand. The only reason I came was to get my mother off my back. I should have run away from Shawn's house in London, found out where my friends were. My ears burned. The queasiness I'd felt in the apartment, when I tried to get some money off Shawn, was turning into all-out nausea. If I didn't get at least a little I'd never be able to eat that pizza.

Fourth time around the block a man came out of one of the old wooden houses between the brick apartment buildings and walked right toward me, his collar up, his hands in his pockets. "What you want?" he asked.

"Don," I said. "You know him?"

"You think we got drugs in this neighborhood? That what you think? Get outta here. I'll call the cops." He turned back toward the house.

My stomach churned. "Fuck you, man," I said. "I live in this colony."

He turned around. "Colony?"

"What do you care if I want to get high?" I fought a chill.

"Look, here, Abdul," he said. I was ready to jab him in his broad, black face, knock him down and take the money I would need for another dealer. I deserved a few bucks for the trouble he was giving me. "We don't want no Arab druggies moving in here."

"I'm no Arab." He blocked my hand at the wrist and before I knew it, his other fist knocked my stomach straight into my backbone.

By the time I could breathe, I was alone on the street. Now I really needed something for the pain.

I got up and ran, to keep warm, in the direction of the park. Somewhere in this country there would have to be a friendly junkie. Just one bag, and I could go to Europe. Even if I had to jump ship. One of those Greek freighters. I could buy a motorcycle, ride across the border, down through Turkey. Maybe up through Austria and Germany to Amsterdam again. Kunti won't be staying here. There's nothing for her. Even Sheela's going. And she has the money. One day Shawn will be the only one of us left in this country, hoarding gold like Hari, wondering how much money he has to have before he can feel the way I know I'll feel as soon as I can find that Don or some other dealer

11 *The Immigrant Disease*

Hari Pal Singh Gill
Half Moon Bay, California

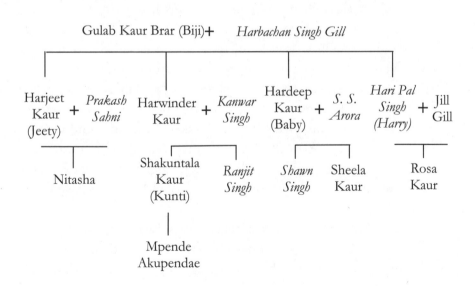

1

COMING TO AMERICA I thought I had escaped with my life. So many miles from my mother and my sisters, I would not be called upon to meddle in mistakes I had not made. Across the Atlantic Harwinder could not come crying, as she had come across the Arabian Sea, only to go back, not taking my advice to leave her brutal husband. Baby would not need me, as soon as my sisters found her a husband, to find her a doctor when she wouldn't stay away from the scum I had warned her about. I was their only brother. They did not have to remind me. And I loved them. I wanted them to be happy. But there were some things I was not responsible for that I could not fix.

New York provides the greatest illusion of freedom in the world. The life of a student, even a graduate student, kept me from realizing for years how carefully my mother and sisters had conspired. I stayed out as late as I wanted, no one to worry about where I was. I slept all day. I could take a hot shower any time, eat breakfast any hour of the day, drink hot, strong coffee. I drank beer from all over the world, American whiskey, scotch. I smoked tobacco, prohibited by our religion, marijuana. I even cut the hair that my mother had painstakingly braided, wrapped and covered when I was a child. And not by a tortured, irreligious process of decision either! Giving up a ton of hair and six yards of gauze did not even *mean* giving up the religion—you can't give up something you're born into—and I never believed in it enough in the first place.

I met Jill in my second year, when I was nearly finished with my master's. What I liked best about her was her reserve. She might be upset to the point of psychosomatic pain, but she would never cry like my sister Jeety, lose her temper like Harwinder, or brood like Baby. Jill was always in control. "Stoic, repressed WASP," she called herself. She was almost as tall as I, and I'm just shy of six feet. She was blonde. She preferred tight, tailored slacks to the baggy pants my mother and sisters always wore. She had breasts the size of apples, not mangos. She could not have been more different.

We used to laugh at the letters I got from my sisters, sometimes my father, asking me if I had found a job, how much I was earning. They had each met families whose daughters were in medical school. They would send me pictures. I could fly to India, Africa, or England to meet her. If I liked her, I could marry her and bring her back.

"Why are Indians in such a hurry to become grandparents, grow old, and die?" she asked.

Years later, on our first trip to Delhi, we couldn't walk down a street in the neighborhood without being asked if we had children. If we said we didn't, shopkeepers I had known since childhood asked, "Why?" After Rosa had been born, family members, people we'd just met at parties all over the world, even total strangers urged us to have another. If a couple's lucky they get a few good years after the children have been born before the questions start again: "Have you found a girl/boy for Pappu? When will s/he get married?"

"In India," I used to till Jill, "I never saw anyone in any hurry to do much else."

In the United States it's just the opposite. Thirty-year-old brides are not considered old, nor is it unusual to honeymoon for five, six years before having children. But if you can get an undergraduate degree in three years, a master's in one, and an executive position before you're twenty-five, you're some kind of hero—if you're a millionaire by the time you're thirty! I'd had the idea, even before I left India, that as soon as I got to New York, the clock would start ticking on my first million. And by the time I turned thirty, I would be a millionaire. All my friends shared the same expectation: "When I make my million, I will marry a lady doctor and retire."

If I had been smart, not merely educated by the best rupees could buy, I might have recognized the conspiracy that put those dreams into my head. Not movies, in which white people lived in huge, immaculate houses and never worked a day of their adventuresome, romantic lives, but my own family. As long as I could remember, my mother had been bragging: "Hari will go to America. We will find him a lady doctor. In America a doctor can make millions."

I was afraid that if I got a job, my sisters' letters would turn into phone calls, maybe even visits, real live lady doctors, smelling of formaldehyde, their hair pulled back in nets. I stayed in graduate school as long as I could.

Remaining in the student stage of life effectively delayed my becoming a householder—in America it's called "prolonging one's adolescence," and it's frowned upon because it doesn't bring in any cash.

One morning of those years of research for my doctoral dissertation, early, the phone rang, and Jill picked it up. "I don't know who it is," she said. "It's not in English."

It was my mother. She had never called before. It was too hard to get through from India, and long distance was expensive. After she had assured me that everything was all right, my father was well, my sisters, I told her I was all right too; it was my secretary who had picked up the phone. "You must have dialed my work number. I start every day by six. In America everyone works long hours, even students."

She was in England helping my youngest sister with her first child, who had just been born. "Send me a ticket. I am coming your side."

I had never asked the family for a cent. My sister Jeety paid for my schooling, the best school in New Delhi—that was the family story. And after she was married, someone else must have paid tuition and room and board for the hostel I lived in at college. In India kids don't get themselves minimum-wage part-time jobs. That's American. In graduate school I got a small stipend for a research assistantship, and I applied for all the scholarships, loans and grants I could get. I could always raise forty-fifty dollars painting apartments or moving furniture. If I'd tried that in New Delhi, the laborers who depend on that kind of work to feed their families would have beaten me up. That is if my family would have allowed me to *appear* for a laborer's job without standing on the street and crying, "Hari has lost his mind! He will have to go to hospital! Good people of New Delhi! Stop him!"

Jill paid the rent and bought the groceries. She would not be doing either if my mother came. I was far from accumulating the million I knew I could make. Scraping together four-five-hundred just to bring my mother into my escape hatch for a month didn't seem possible.

I thought of going to London myself, wondered what a charter flight might cost. But my semester was in full swing. I couldn't go anywhere.

I asked my mother to give the phone to Baby. "Baby? I wish I could, but I just can't. Do you know how much a round-trip ticket costs? I just paid tuition."

"Do not worry," Baby said. "I will handle it."

Not another week went by before she called with my mother's arrival time and flight number, compliments of my brother-in-law S. S. Arora, who apparently had more money than he knew what to do with.

Jill had to move out in a hurry. We hid all the stuff she wouldn't need and hauled the rest to a friend's apartment. Space was at such a premium in Manhattan that even half the rent could not console Jill's temporary roommate, especially as my mother stayed, month after month. Jill had to spend the money we would have lived on to rent her own, separate apartment. At least that gave us a place to have sex while my mother was in town.

Not that I hadn't missed my mother. In those first few years I'd walk down a street, and the diesel fumes would flash me back into a cloud spewed by a rattling, dilapidated lorry passing the veranda of our Delhi house. I could almost hear the tinkling of the bangles on my mother's wrist as she waved the exhaust away, making a music I had rarely heard since leaving Delhi. Or I might pass a chestnut vendor and the wood smoke no one could escape in Delhi would pull my heart back to the sunny days and cold, crisp nights I had spent in the courtyard figuring out equations while my mother bargained with vegetable hawkers, shouted instructions to our servant or gossiped with my sisters. There had even been moments, brief and usually when I was sick, when I wished that I had never left, that I had gone to graduate school in Delhi—or Bombay, where I would live in an entirely different city but still be able to come home and listen to my mother's gossip while I stuffed myself on her butter chicken.

The thrill of seeing her again, healthy, as I'd left her, stayed with me all winter. Her reaction to the tallest buildings in the world amused me, and sitting down to her spicy meals every night consoled me for the distance between Jill and me. But I paid for that delicious cooking, that odd feeling of comfort. In New York I had developed a sense of privacy. That was gone. Biji listened every time I answered the phone, stared whenever I did simple things that she had never seen me do, like making myself a cup of coffee. Black, no sugar. "Child, this black coffee will make you sick."

"No, Biji, I'm perfectly healthy."

It was strange, this combination of annoyance and comfort. When I was in India I had only been aware of the annoyance. Biji made me feel like a kid again, illogically secure, with nothing to do but pass my exams and hang out with my friends. Except that in New York *I* was the one paying for the groceries, scraping together enough to cover the rent. It cleaned me out when I had to buy her a coat, and every time she said she wanted something for the house in Delhi—a toaster, a television—my heart rose to my throat. It was difficult for students to get credit cards in those days. But a worse problem was the fact that in New York my mother was alone, with no one to stop by. I felt guilty, as I had never felt in India, every time I went out. I tried studying at home, but she kept interrupting: did I want eggs for breakfast, a cup of tea; did I see the ad for cleaning liquid on TV?

I could not allow her to go out alone. She didn't know the neighborhoods, and she was small; gold glittered on her arm. Nor did she feel comfortable. It was cold. She knew no one but me. It was not the life she had been used to.

Jill kept asking me when I was going to introduce her. "When a guy won't introduce you to his parents," she said, "it's time to get the sexy clothes out of the back of the closet and say 'Nothing' when the guy who sells you coffee asks you what you're doing Saturday night."

"You don't know what you're saying," I tried to explain. "If I invite you over, my mother will suspect that you and I are getting married."

"Well?"

I hadn't thought of that. I was in no hurry. "You have no idea what she's like when she's upset. Crying, fainting, threatening, not cooking. She'll make me promise not to see you, and I don't want to have to lie about that."

"She doesn't know you're seeing me now. *That's* not a lie?"

My mother was as bad as Jill. "Don't you have any friends? Have you told them not to come? Are you ashamed of your mother?"

I had no choice but to invite the crowd Jill and I hung out with. Americans brought their boyfriends or girlfriends; Indians and Jill came alone. My mother assumed that the Americans were married, felt sorry that the families of my Indian friends had not found them wives. The truth was my friends were afraid that if they brought their lovers, my mother would somehow get the information onto the grapevine, and their families would come to know.

Some of those boys eventually got up the courage, told their parents and married Americans or Indians of different communities. Some broke up, flew to India and came back with a wife.

"Such a shame," my mother commented. "One girl so tall and ugly that no one will marry her."

My friends, those who could understand her Punjabi, laughed. "That's Jill," they said. "Don't you like her?"

"Let's eat," I said.

Jill opened the silverware drawer.

"What does it matter if I like her?" my mother answered. "There is no need for a boy's mother to like all of his friends. Now, the girl he marries, I must like."

When Jill couldn't find forks and knives in their usual drawers, she said, "Harry, where'd you put the silverware?"

I signed my name, "Harry Gill" in America. It was easier. I didn't tell my mother. I didn't tell her, either, about Jill's invitations to dinner, to a musical or sightseeing out of the city to Bear Mountain or Jones Beach. I thought she would stay a month, maybe two. But Baby had bought her an open ticket, and the standard tourist visa was good for four months. "Why should I hurry?" she asked. "Even in India your father was always out. I hardly ever saw him. How can he miss me now?"

His letters were pathetic: *once the father of four, now I am alone.*

I could not afford to bring him over, though his letters toyed with the idea of retiring so he could spend more time with "the children." Even then I knew he meant me. Like many Indians of the generation before him, he believed he'd given up his daughters when he got them married. Jill, in her new apartment, wearing sexy clothing I had not seen for years, assumed that my mother would be staying illegally, especially after Biji made me get her four-month visa extended. "What's it going to be?" Jill asked. "Do I get to hang out with you and your mother? Or do I cry my eyes out, go into therapy, and ask the guy at the coffee shop when he gets off work?"

She was not the ugly girl my mother saw in her long blonde hair and slim white legs. She had the flawless complexion and China blue eyes of a New York model. She could have any man she wanted, I knew that, and I had always been a little flattered that she wanted me. I had to give in to at least one dinner or Jill might never forgive me. But I was afraid that if I agreed to dinner at Jill's favorite Indian restaurant, my mother would stay beyond her unrenewable eight months, raising the money from my sisters to bring my father over, and forbidding, on the pain of hunger, any further communication with the "tall, white-haired girl too ugly to marry."

Instead she told me it was time to go. She had things to do. She left me at the airport with this advice: "When a boy goes to America, he must take care. These Americans are clever. I have seen that on this country's TV. They will bewitch you, and you must not ever take their part against the family. Do not go to restaurants with women; do not invite them to your parties. People will say that you are having an affair, and it will be much more difficult for your sisters or me to find you a lady doctor."

I should not have reassured her. I should have told her not to waste her time looking for that doctor. Separation had made Jill and me fonder of each other than we'd ever been, in spite of Jill's friend at the coffee shop. But it was easier to nod and put my mother on the plane. I had already contracted the immigrant disease, though I had not yet learned how to stand up for myself like an American.

All the time I spent delaying my entry into the workforce should have been my first clue. I would not accumulate that million by my thirtieth birthday. My second should have been the fact that I had entered the workforce at all. I got an excellent job, in pharmaceuticals, at a salary I'd only been able to imagine as a graduate student in a city of high rents. I was ready for the whole American dream— corporate success, a house. I was ready to get married. I wrote Jeety, thinking, as the eldest, she would be the one to arrange it:

My dearest sister,

I am fine. I hope you all are well, Prakash Papa, Nitasha, your mother-in-law, your brothers- and sisters-in-law and their children.

Jill, back with me in an apartment we had moved to in New Jersey, said, "Just write the letter, Harry. I'm not outrunning any biological clock here waiting for you to get through the Academy Award speech."

Filling most of an aerogramme with greetings to Jeety's extended family saved me from going into too much detail about the American girl I wanted to marry. I closed by saying I would be glad to fly to India as soon as the company I had joined would allow me my two weeks, probably around Christmas. It would not be necessary for the family to arrange a meeting with a girl. I had found a girl, and I would be bringing her to India to meet my father. I had known Jill for several years, even Biji knew her.

I should have known my great escape was about to face a prolonged invasion. I had preferred to see my mother's visit as an isolated incident; in reality it had been my family's reconnaissance to determine how hostile the environment might be, how resistant American forces. In retrospect I do not think I ever portrayed American life in its full hostility. No one in my family had ever had to earn in America or pay expenses. True, even in New York it was easier to break even than in India, and there were so many more things an American could do for income. But expenses were another thing, especially in New York. Despite the homeless—fewer and more isolated than the whole families that put up shanties on the streets of every Indian city—as far as my mother could tell, every American went from a clean hospital to a warm apartment; everyone worked or studied; anyone could get anything available in the hundreds of stores that surrounded us—and in New York everything is available. If I had been able to show my family the ceiling that even I could not see, especially designed to filter out women like my sisters and their daughters; or if they had ever seen the dealers on the corners of the neighborhoods their children would one day struggle to afford, I might have left them with a more realistic impression of the richest country in the world. But at the time even I thought immigrants could live better here than anywhere else in the world. I was determined to rise high enough in the company to accumulate at least a million, at least in assets by the time I turned forty.

Baby called a week before Jill and I had planned to fly to India and said that everything was taken care of. Everyone had come to London, all of them—my mother and father, all three sisters, even the children they had given birth to while I was in America—and they were all planning to cross the Atlantic for my wedding. Jill called her mother and her sisters, and I scrambled to find someone to read our holy book.

On the coldest day of the year my family descended on the house Jill and I had just moved into. Jill dubbed them "The Golden Horde" because wherever we went there were twelve of us—seven adults and five children—and because they had come for a wedding, my mother and sisters had worn all the gold they could deck their arms, necks, ears and fingers with. Even their Punjabi suits and saris were embroidered with gold. Jill got gold too, a necklace, earrings and bangles, and on the morning of the wedding my sisters tied a red and gold sari around her.

The family walked Jill and me around the holy book in our new living room, no furniture to move. Then we partied. Jill's family went home, and Jill and I hid out at a ski resort in northern New Jersey. "Let's just stay," she said. "The house is under siege, and we'll be taken as hostages if we go back." At the time the American embassy in Iran was occupied; pictures of Americans, blindfolded, surrounded by brown-skinned terrorists, filled the papers and the television screen.

"Now be nice," I said. We had to go back—to drive my sisters to the malls, to New York and Washington, to restaurants, finally to the airport, where Jill suggested we spend at least one night—so much more private was JFK International than our first house, where my mother and father waited for news that my sisters' luggage had made it onto the plane.

There were happy moments in that house, dishes I had forgotten, the roses my father planted in the garden. I heard the names of uncles and aunts I had forgotten, and when their children got married, I sent telegrams and spoke to them again. I learned details about my parents' first years in New Delhi I had never known in India.

But Jill, even I, had always preferred the nuclear to the extended family. Partially it was because nobody else we knew had parents sliding into the car every Saturday to help them choose couches, tables, chairs for what even my sisters had called "our house."

"That's cultural," I realized. "Every house in the family is referred to as 'our house.'"

"Really? Even that big house in Bombay where Jeety is so miserable living with all of her husband's brothers and their families?"

How to explain: even my sister, in a joint family in Bombay, would have preferred a single family house, only her husband and daughter?

"Well, no," I said. "That's my sister's house. The sisters' houses belong to the sisters' husbands' families. It's only the brother's house that is home to all of his family."

It had never occurred to me that my parents might ever voluntarily move to a place with which they were thoroughly unfamiliar, where people stared at my father's pastel turbans and my mother's bright silks surreptitiously, the way Americans were taught *not* to look at people who are different; where my parents could not get up from the family room, closed up, as our Delhi house had never been, and walk to their brothers' and sisters' houses, to the taxi stand, where they could get a taxi to the shops, anywhere in Delhi, where they could go every morning to the neighborhood Gurdwara, to hear the priests read from the holy book and sing Sikh hymns. As they grew older, my father stayed with us while my mother relieved her boredom by traveling to London and Nairobi. My sister Baby kept up a lively Indian party circuit. In Nairobi the Indian community was also large, and Harwinder lived in almost complete isolation from ethnic Africans.

This went on for years, the entire course of my married life, what they call in India the householder period, which I thought would be different in America. I worked long hours trying to prove myself as first a corporate man and then a businessman in the country I had adopted. I became a citizen. It was not just to sponsor my parents for green cards that would make it easier for them to travel. It was also out of a commitment, like the commitment I had made to Jill. Love America and I would one day see that million.

Ortho passed me over for promotion. More than once. It took me years to figure out: the reason I was not considered executive material was that I did not follow American football, baseball or basketball. I could have managed tennis if I'd had the time. I missed cricket. I did not play golf. I could not hold my liquor either like these broad Americans, who had developed a tolerance partying in American fraternities. That might have been all right if I had been a woman. Women were not expected to talk sports, drink profusely, and bond in the locker room. The graduate school experience could be no substitute, I learned, for gentlemen's C's on the undergraduate level. In fact the PhD may have been one of my drawbacks.

So when my sisters sent my nieces and nephews for their undergraduate degrees, I thought they were doing the right thing. Jill was not so sure: "Doesn't India have colleges? I mean you can spell twice as good as me, and your math!"

I sent Jeety's daughter Nitasha applications for Rutgers, Princeton, NYU, Penn and Columbia. She got into Rutgers. Jeety wanted me to keep an eye on her, to make sure she studied, got into medical school, and married a Punjabi boy.

"But she can't live with us," Jill said. "Are you going to teach her how to drive? Buy a car so she can get to class? Pay for her insurance?"

I got her a good room in a dormitory, with nice roommates, who would help her to make friends. American friends, I thought, would open her up to American life, in a way that no classes in sociology or history could do, show her how to work at an east-coast pace, how to compete with kids who had been raised in well-to-do American suburbs, how to develop her ambition, so that she would always succeed at well-paying jobs. And no one would have to find her a husband. She was beautiful. I had a soft spot in my heart for this, my eldest sister's child, the first of her generation. She was shy, I thought, diffident about the college social scene. That was good. She did not go to parties, did not follow American rock groups or spend hundreds of dollars on concerts or clubs, didn't drink, smoke or overeat. She was as far as I could tell a virgin. If she had been a little more studious or if she held down a part-time job instead of spending every weekend that first year shopping and watching television with us, she would have been a splendid role model for Rosa. Jill called her immature. When her best friend from India moved to Canada, Nitasha stopped spending holidays with us.

"She is the best friend I will ever have in life," Nitasha told me when I asked if she had made good friends at Rutgers. "No one will ever understand me quite so well, and I will never understand these Americans."

Though I had not made my million, my doctorate in chemical engineering *had* gotten me a job, a house, savings I could use to buy my own business. Even if Nitasha did not have the grades, test scores or desire to get into medical school, she could still find a job, fall in love with a guy as tolerant and hard-working as Jill, and make a life for herself. But somehow for my sisters' kids the American dream did not take.

Harwinder's daughter came, also went to Rutgers, and took a job even lower paying than Nitasha's. My sister urged me to get her a job at Ortho, but my influence was not worth anything by that time, and Kunti herself said she did not want to join the white male establishment. Even before that I knew that she was not destined to make a million in America.

When Baby sent her son and daughter to her husband's sister on the west coast, I was secretly relieved. If she had sent them to us, Jill would have said, "No way," and I would not have been able to say no. Then when Sheela took a job in a restaurant in California instead of moving in with us to go to a community college, my sisters blamed me. They blamed me for Nitasha's refusal to get married, for Kunti's promiscuity, pregnancy and poverty. Guilt might not have bothered me—after all, my nieces' lives were none of my business, as they themselves frequently reminded me—if I had not been called upon so often to bail them out. Then on the night my brother-in-law Kanwar called from a public phone in New Brunswick, I thought the family had really hit bottom. No one had even telephoned to tell me he was coming. "Brother," he slurred, "you have not done your duty by this family. Now you must drive to this place before someone hits me on the head and steals my—"

"Where are you? It sounds like a local call."

"How am I to know where I am? I will wait for you in one hotel on the corner, this T. G. I. Friday. Kindly come. I have little luggage. I have just arrived—"

"Where is Kunti?" I asked. "Does she know you're here?"

"I have no daughter. I will wait for you in T. G. I. Okay."

He hung up. Jill stirred in the bed. "It's four o'clock in the morning."

"How can a T. G. I. Friday's be open," I asked, "and in what city? What state?"

I called Kunti. "Did you know your father was here?"

"How could I have missed it? He beat me up."

"Where is he? He wants me to pick him up."

"I don't know." She started crying. I couldn't make any sense out of anything she tried to say.

"Is there a T. G. I. Friday's in New Brunswick?" I asked. "Where is it?"

Her boyfriend, whom I had never met, gave me peremptory directions, as if *I* had asked *him* to take care of my aging brother-in-law, the least he could do, I thought, for fathering the bastard's grandchild. But if I knew Kanwar he had beaten up the boyfriend too. I pulled a pair of pants and sweater over my pajamas and went out in the cold to pick up my brother-in-law. Then, until he passed out on the couch, my mother and father greeting the dawn beside him, I had to put up with his side of the story.

"I'm going to look for a business in California," I told Jill. It was not so much the responsibility of looking after my sisters' daughters, not even their failures to succeed at the professions my sisters had imagined for them. Jill and I had been talking about California ever since I decided to give up the pharmaceutical industry. I had somehow lost my thirties, but I knew if I could buy or start a company of my own, I could make a million by the time I turned fifty. Jill said, "If it doesn't matter where we live, we may as well live somewhere warm." Everyone we knew would go to California in a minute. California was the end of the rainbow, ever since the prospectors risked their lives and families for gold.

Perhaps it began with the stress of Kanwar's sudden appearance in the middle of the night, the birth of a great-grandchild before any one of their grandchildren could be married. Doctors blamed his age.

My father's health declined so rapidly that shortly after Harwinder came to help Kunti with the baby, my father went into the hospital. When he did not rally, Baby came from England. I did all I could to get him the best medical care in the world. I would have flown him to Texas for a transplant if his kidneys had not given out before I could find him a heart.

With my father no longer in the world, the memories came back: I'm sitting beside him on the men's side of the Gurdwara, never imagining that I might one day have to lead him by the hand into a Gurdwara in New Jersey, in a converted split level, simply to pray among strangers, people the family would not even notice had they never left a country full of friends and relatives. I sit beside him smooth faced as I was when I had been a boy, my short hair covered with his handkerchief instead of the fresh, starched turban he wore. I remember him announcing, strangely exhilarated, at my graduation party in India, that I would study engineering, not pure chemistry, which I had been good at, because a boy in the family must study a practical subject so as to get a job in a government ministry or big corporation. And I did, sometimes wondering what I might have been able to do with something I had loved. How proud he was, years later, prouder by far than the truth would ever let me be, that I had landed a job with a company that makes birth control pills available all over the world. I remember how serious he was throughout my wedding, speaking in low tones with Jill about the kind of furniture we would eventually fill the house with, the renovations needed in the kitchen, the landscaping we could not enhance until the winter was over, so that Jill had to whisper to me, as he had been whispering with her, "I think your father is trying to tell me something about homemaking." I would never shake from my mind how sad his face could be, after a day of television and my mother, when I would come in late; how guilty it made me feel, then how perceptibly his face, pulled into a scowl by wrinkles, brightened as we sat over our dinner—chicken my mother had made, okra, bitter gourd or cauliflower.

If I had only made him happy. Despite the engineering I did not particularly like, the job I could only make so much money persisting in, I hadn't even tried.

I never really knew him. He was rarely home when I was growing up, and when he was, he closed himself up in the drawing room while I was kept out in the courtyard with my mother and sisters. I must have taken after him because even before I moved into the hostel at college, I hardly came home myself. We might have had our best contact through the aerogrammes we exchanged quite regularly while I was in graduate school. But his English was so formal, like the civil servant he was, informing an inferior of the state of things in the field: *as per your mother, be informed that her prognosis remains positive. Loneliness is there, with the children so far away, but be assured that she will come your side as soon as you are settled.*

If I had settled any sooner, I might have had the time to know him better, but even after he had settled himself into the guest room of our New Jersey house, I went out early, in a hurry, before I could eat the breakfast my mother had prepared for me. I came home after seven. Instead of talking with him after dinner, I sat down with my work until I fell asleep. Sometimes I worked weekends. I thought that if I put in the hours, I would be promoted to the big shot in America that all of my friends who had stayed in India had become—army generals, heads of government ministries, CEO's. I would be making my father happy, I thought, happier than he would be if I sat down and gossiped with him, as he could never stand to hear my mother and my sisters gossip. At least not talking with him he would never know how little I agreed with the view of the world that had brought him such pain.

My sisters stayed for three-four months after my father's funeral. With four women lying about on the carpet, drying their hair, sighing, reminiscing in a language only a fraction of the housing market could understand, the real estate agent we were dealing with discouraged us from showing the house. Our kitchen smelled of curry, not the chocolate chip cookies or at least the baking stick of cinnamon the agent had recommended. Suitcases lined the walls; towels dried on the deck railings; the telephone was always ringing. On weekends Kunti and the baby joined us, Nitasha. Shawn flew out from California to lie around the house for the summer before college. Someone had to comfort my mother. She was inconsolable. I had never thought my mother and father *had* much of a relationship. She always spoke to him quite harshly, and he avoided her as best he could, even after retirement, even shut up in the same suburban house. She thought nothing of leaving him to visit my sisters for months at a time. But with him gone, she had no one, she said, and in a sense it was true. Without my sisters, she would have been alone all day. Jill worked, and Rosa was in school; in summertime she went to camp. "With an only child," Jill used to say, "you've got to provide interaction with other children. Essentially, we've got to buy her friends."

I wish I could have bought my mother the kind of constant interaction she enjoyed in India. Baby took her back to London. Biji spent time, as had been her custom, in Baby's house, then in Harwinder's in Nairobi; finally she went to India, where Jeety left Bombay to stay with her in Delhi.

Jill and I packed up the clothing, toiletries and odds and ends that she had left in our guest room and took them with us across the country. I gave up the dream of founding a whole new venture on my own and bought a franchise. Rosa says it was the name Midas that attracted me, especially in the Golden State. But if I could turn everything I touched, I would not be struggling to turn my initial investment into enough profit to buy out the competition in a state where the only salt laid down to melt the snow and ice and corrode the mufflers I replace lies in the mountains a day's drive and the driver's choice away. But there are a lot of cars in California. I look forward to a million, easy, if only in the business, the house, the stocks I got when I left Ortho, by the time I'm sixty.

2

On a cold day in January the last of my sisters' children came to America. Were it not for my mother we would not have known. She spoke to each of my sisters at least once a week, and after Harwinder told her that Ranjit had passed through London and was already in New Brunswick, Biji called Kunti to chide him for not calling. He asked her to send a few hundred.

My mother had gotten smart over the years. She called Baby in London: "How much did you give him?"

"Don't send him anything," Biji told me. "He will only drink it." She had seen him in action in Africa. "If he were this side, that might be different."

No, I prayed, no. Not in the same house with my daughter.

My mother was always trying to convince the kids to move to California. She kept in touch with a journalist Nitasha had met when she was visiting, but all of her interest could not get Nitasha and the journalist together. In fact, I think the journalist married someone else, and Nitasha told my mother, "If he's that much of a hypocrite, I wouldn't have been able to spend the rest of my life with him anyway." Kunti said that she would move to California in a minute, but the father of her baby threatened to follow her and kidnap the child if she tried to leave New Brunswick. I was secretly relieved that Ranjit had admission to Rutgers and not one of the California campuses. Harwinder told my mother she had falsified his records. He had never completed his examinations, and he'd spent five years doing nothing but riding across Europe and Africa on motorcycles. Shawn was planning to work on Wall Street after getting his degree from Harvard, a natural move, considering his major. Only Sheela had been out here when we had arrived, three-hundred-fifty miles to the south. She came to see us on her way back, first to Massachusetts to stay with Shawn, then to London. "Then I'm going to stay with Aunt Jeety for a while," she told us. "To go to college in India."

"India?" my mother said. "India is all dirt and trouble. We got out of that place."

"That's what my mother says," she said, smiling gently into the iced tea Rosa had made for her. A gallon of milk sat warming on the table. Even after twenty years, on and off in the United States, my mother could not imagine tea without milk and sugar, let alone cold.

Sheela seemed to have achieved some kind of enlightenment working for a Buddhist-Christian Chinese restaurateur in the San Fernando Valley and living with a Jewish family after Arora's family had kicked her out. It seemed to me, it seemed to my mother, Sheela's mother, even Shawn a waste to leave the land of opportunity just when Sheela had saved enough to afford in-state tuition at Berkeley, UCLA or UC Santa Barbara—wherever her high school grades and test scores could get her in. "I want to live in the country of my origins," she argued, "at least as long as it takes to get an undergraduate degree. After that I'll decide. I've got a British passport, an American green card. I can live anywhere."

I saw a lot of truth to that. Unlike my mother, unlike even me, Sheela had either developed an appreciation for the family's diaspora or inherited her versatility because of it. On her way back to London she was going to see all of the cousins. She invited Rosa, "You can stay with me and Shawn in Cambridge. We'll drive down to see Nitasha, Kunti and Ranjit. Do you know how long it's been since all of us have been together?"

"For me, never," Rosa said. "Dad, can I go?"

You know the family's gone down when you feel you have to protect your daughter from your own nephews and nieces. "Let's get them all out here," I said. "For your graduation."

"That's a year and a half from now!"

I thank God I did not send her.

The first call, after Sheela had been in Massachusetts for two-three weeks, had nothing to do with Ranjit. It was Nitasha's mother. "How could you let my daughter shift to that cold place? You have a family business. You could have given her a job!"

"What cold place?" I said. "Where are you calling from?"

"India! Nitasha called! From Canada!"

"It's the first I've heard of it."

It was the night after the kids had met—in Kunti's apartment in New Brunswick. I pieced the details together: in the morning Nitasha moved out of her Jersey City apartment and spent the day crossing New York State with her friend, Lalita. Only after she had reached the motel Lalita's mother and father had bought in Niagara Falls did Nitasha call Bombay and tell Jeety and Prakash: she was tired of living alone in Jersey City trying to support herself with a job she couldn't stand. In Canada she had been approved for immigration, and Lalita had offered her a place to live.

"The children don't consult me," I said. "Give me Lalita's phone number. I'll call her."

What could I do? Nitasha had no experience installing mufflers, and with Jill and Rosa I had all the office help I could use. If she wanted to come to California and find her own job, she could stay with us. What choice did I have if I wanted to appease my sister? But Nitasha didn't want to come.

"Thanks, Hari," she said. "But I've been planning this move for some time. Ever since I was there visiting you, actually. I know what I'm doing. Tell Mummy."

My mother was standing by the phone in the kitchen. "That girl had Nitasha bewitched long before she came to this country," she said.

"What?"

"She is the kind of girl you see in men's pajamas. It was a mistake of her mother to allow the girls to become fast friends in Bombay even."

"She got an offer to manage her friend's motel," I said. "That's not bad. It's better than struggling all by yourself, even if it *does* get colder in the winter. Maybe she'll meet a guy in Canada. She's not too old. Americans get married in their eighties. There was that woman in England—she had a baby at fifty."

"What does it matter if the most important relationship in her life is not a man?" Rosa argued, passing through the kitchen to pull a Coke out of the refrigerator. "At least she *has* a relationship."

"What makes you think it is so important to have a relationship?" I asked. "If you do well in school, if you get a good job—"

"Don't tell her that," Jill said, close behind Rosa. "She'll drop out and run off with a sheet-metal worker just to prove you wrong."

"What do you have against sheet-metal workers?" Rosa protested, slamming the refrigerator door.

But there was worse. After Nitasha called her mother in India, she called Kunti. Kunti thought her brother had spent the night at Nitasha's. Nitasha thought he had gone home to Kunti's. "He's probably in bed with some girl," I told Nitasha. When Ranjit didn't show up the next night, Kunti called the police, the hospitals, then me. I asked my mother if Ranjit had called. "He never calls," she said. "None of the children calls."

"If he's on his way here," I told Kunti, "it could take him weeks. We took a week driving out from Jersey, and we had a car." I made her promise not to call her mother. What could my sister do, halfway across the world? Kunti's take on her brother's absence would only upset Harwinder, and Ranjit had probably merely wandered off.

"That boy is always disappearing," my mother said. "The first time, he tried to get on a ship in Mombasa. The captain was a good man. He called Nairobi. Kanwar drove all the way across Kenya and brought him back. He had to go into the hospital with liver problems, or they would have sent him here. One time he turned up in Italy. He called and asked Harwinder to send money. He called Baby once from France. Arora told him to go home, get a job if he wouldn't go to school. He got sick at that time too, left his motorcycle with a boy he met in Europe. He never saw it again. Harwinder got smart after that. When he called again she sent a non-refundable ticket."

But Harwinder called, and when she asked to speak to Ranjit, Kunti could not help but tell her that she hadn't heard from him in days.

I got a call from Nairobi: "What are you doing to find my son? He is missing, like those children on the milk cartons in your crazy country! I did not believe it could happen in America . . ."

I tried to tell her he had not been gone long enough to be considered missing. And Africa, where he had taken off before, was much more dangerous, or so my sister had always insisted, with thieves and African nationalists ready to kill Asians for accumulating millions in East Africa. Not that spaces between New Jersey and California did not have their share of thieves and nationalists too, anti-African, some of them, anti-Asian, who would kill a man for bringing his brown skin into the New World.

I waited for a few more days, calling Kunti every day to ask if Ranjit had shown up. I called Shawn in Massachusetts, even Nitasha in Canada. Funny I did not think I could count on them to call me as soon as he turned up. I called London and told Baby if she heard from him to contact me. Hadn't he resisted his mother's sending him to Jersey? Hadn't he threatened to run away instead of attending college? I called the New Brunswick police: "I'm Harry Gill, the boy's maternal uncle, his eldest male relative in the United States." What a jerk I sounded like. Seniority means nothing in American families. Ranjit's own sister, twenty-seven years old, was an adult herself, a mother, Ranjit Singh's next of kin, as they called it. If the cops found anything, they'd call *her*.

"What shall I do?" I asked my mother. "What good is all the money in the world if I can't find my own sister's child?"

"All the money in his father's pockets turned him into a boy who thinks he can have anything," she said. "He will call. When he needs something."

Kanwar called me too, every time he got drunk. "What have you done to my son, you bastard!"

I hung up without talking to him, every time.

"Serves him well," my mother said.

Despite the tough talk she had always favored as the first child of a large, wealthy family, she worried too. She called Harwinder every day, called Kunti, Nitasha, even Shawn. She opened her holy book more often than usual. While I paid a monthly retainer to an investigation company I knew little about, she sent Jeety to astrologers in India. Each gave a different report: *He will be all right. Harwinder must fast for him and wear a special ring the astrologer has sold to Jeety. He has given in to his desires. The consequence of living by the passions is not good. He is all right. He is wandering this earth. He is begging for his food, sleeping in the open like a holy man. We must accept his disappearance in this world. He is all right. He has been released from all desires.*

My investigator checked the homeless shelters in New Jersey and the major cities. It was winter. Ranjit would not survive outdoors the way he had in Africa, even in Europe. The agency checked hospital records, questioned dealers, called me every time a brown-skinned man, five-foot-eleven, in his twenties, uncircumcised, no distinguishing features, was brought into a morgue.

Most of them were identified even before the coroner could send me a photograph. I could tell nothing from a picture anyway. I had not seen Ranjit since he was three years old, when he had come for my wedding almost twenty years ago. All I had to go on were the photographs my mother showed me. I could not help but remember the role that stress had played in the death of my father, and I was afraid of killing her with a picture of a casualty of the third generation. I sent the coroner's photographs to Shawn. I would have sent them to Kunti, but I didn't think she could handle identifying a dead body. Even I was repulsed. I could not bear even the thought, and looking at a corpse, even my father, when I had to slip a turban onto his head for the funeral director in New Jersey, had repelled me to the point of dizziness. And then I realized it was just my father, and I gave the turban to the undertaker. I could not see to slip it on my father's head.

Most of the photographs came back: "No. His face is not so broad . . . He doesn't have freckles, or whatever that is . . . His hair is not curly . . . He has all his teeth."

Once he could not say. "The expression is not his. It's so rigid."

"It's a picture of a corpse, Shawn."

"I don't know."

"Can you fly to Miami? I'll send you the ticket."

"Yeah," he said. "It could be him."

"So this is it," said Jill.

"Yes. But don't tell my mother. She'll tell my sister and Kunti, and until we claim the body—"

"'Nuff said."

I arranged to reach Miami close to the same time as Shawn's flight got in and met him at his gate. He looked professional, in a gray suit and white shirt, the tie rolled up in his pocket, but for the gleam of gel oiling his black hair and the overabundance of scent he had drenched his body with. I was proud of this nephew. He was the only of my sisters' children who seemed capable of making it in this country, millions maybe, with the best qualifications he could have and a job guaranteed to bring him enough money to buy a big house in the suburbs, any college in the country for any kids he might have, a comfortable retirement for his parents—whatever he wanted for the rest of his life.

We took a cab directly from the airport. Florida was so green compared even to Northern California, so lush. I could see that even in the dark. The palm trees sported bigger tops, the shrubs all blooming with red, orange, yellow hibiscus and bougainvillea. "Grim business," I said. I could not imagine how morticians got to sleep.

"I spent every holiday with him," Shawn reminisced, as we sped down a highway. "We used to ride his motorcycle around his house in Nairobi. When my parents would let me, I got one too. We took a trip through Europe."

"I know," I said.

"That trip was the beginning of the end."

"Was he into drugs?" I asked. "Even then?"

"He got high," Shawn said. "Everybody smokes marijuana. We used to raid his dad's liquor. It's an illness. My frat did a program on it. Some poor bastards get it. Some can drink all night, then leave it alone."

Luckily we were able to get into the morgue that evening. An attendant—no nonsense, black, in a T-shirt and jeans, he could have been any city worker—rolled a gurney into a room, garishly lit with overhead fluorescents, overcooled. Without saying a word he unzipped the bag that covered a human body and revealed a face, gray-brown, the mouth gaping with yellow teeth, a black tongue. I shivered and had to look away. Shawn's mouth broke into a grimace. He shook his head.

"Cuban," the attendant said. "Or Guatemalan. South American guy."

Shawn nodded, tears drying on his lashes. "Thank God," he whispered.

On the warm, humid street I hailed another taxi. "Airport," I told the driver.

"I thought we'd stay closer to the beach," Shawn said.

"I'm going to try to catch the red-eye."

"Tonight? We haven't even eaten."

"Can you eat after that?"

"The food on the plane is terrible. I thought we'd stay."

"What for? It wasn't him." If it had been, we'd have had to decide whether to ship the body to New Jersey or bring Kunti down and cremate it in Miami.

"I like Florida," Shawn said. "I used to drive to Lauderdale for a kind of spring break thing."

"Don't you have to work? I've got to get back."

"You work for yourself. You can take off any time you want."

"I never worked so hard when I was working for someone else."

"Everybody works so hard in this country," Shawn said. "I didn't realize it in college. I mean, college was easy. Ever since I moved to New York I have no life. I get home at nine, ten o'clock. I haven't had a vacation—"

"Well, you haven't worked for a year yet."

"I don't know if I can take a year. There's a bank in London I think I'd like to try."

"To try? A job is not a consumer item, Shawn. Besides, you can't make much money in England. It's practically a welfare state. And London's expensive."

"I can live at home."

"How old are you? Why would you want to live off your parents?"

"I won't be living off them. I'll be working. I just won't have to pay rent. Do you know how much I'm paying in New York?"

"Shawn," it occurred to me. "Were you really fooled by that picture? Did you mislead me just to get a trip to Florida?"

"How can you say that?" His eyes glassed over. "I didn't *want* to fly here. I don't *ever* want to walk into a room and see my cousin on a slab."

Could it have been him, I wondered; had he changed so much in death that Shawn couldn't tell, didn't want to? "Sorry," I said.

"It just seems like such a waste of a good trip," he said. "Can you lend me some cash?"

"If you don't have the money, how can you stay?"

I got a flight to San Francisco and left Shawn at the terminal. I don't know whether he flew back to New York or took a cab to a hotel on the beach. I didn't pay for it. I slipped him a fifty for dinner. I was disappointed. He was the only kid in the family who might have made a million before his thirtieth birthday. But his idea of success revolved around resorts, it seemed, travel, luxury hotels, good food. I liked those things too, everybody did, but I had to work for them. I'd never had a family, like Shawn's, that was able to foot the bill.

I would have to decide what to do in the future, if another body turned up in Chicago or Dallas. Fly Shawn out on his own? I could catch the next flight if the body turned out to be Ranjit's. If Shawn moved to London it would be a lot harder to fly him to a morgue. Kunti would *have* to do it.

I was not surprised when Harwinder told my mother she was coming, and a little later when she called from Kunti's. She asked me to send them tickets—her, Kunti and the child. "Doesn't Kunti have to work?" I asked.

"She can get the same job in California. We cannot stay here. The boy keeps threatening to take the child."

"He has a car," I said. "Even if you leave, he can drive out here after you."

"That is what Kunti says. She is afraid. I have never seen her so afraid, especially in the dark that took my son! It is her brother's disappearance. Children are disappearing all of the time in this country. I never thought. I cannot leave her here alone. She must have someone to watch Mpende. What to do?"

I couldn't answer her. I had moved to California so I wouldn't have to get up in the night and rescue my family when they couldn't deal with their own problems. But Harwinder's problems had become insurmountable. I had to offer her a fresh start. I promised her three tickets. Jill was irate. "How is dragging us down going to help Harwinder and Kunti? Your mother is at the end of her life. She doesn't deserve the stress of coping with a control freak, a paranoid, and a spoiled brat, in generational order. Rosa wants to go out all the time as it is. You don't think a spoiled four-year-old isn't going to drive her out of the house even more than you have?"

"I have?"

"With your insistence that she study all the time, work. She's a kid, Harry. In order to learn how to work, kids have to play."

"These kids play too much if you ask me," I said. "We'll get Kunti a job, even Harwinder. We'll get them their own apartment."

"Who's going to look after the kid if they're both working?"

"Day care," I said. "Maybe my mother can do it."

"Your mother is too old to run after a toddler."

What choice did I have?

As it turned out even Harwinder and Kunti had no choice. They tried packing quickly, secretly, but the baby's father saw the bags— my sisters all carried enormous bags on their trips from country to country. He confronted them, accused them of planning exactly what they had planned. He stayed home for several days; Harwinder stayed with him, for fear that he might take the kid. Kunti tried to go to work, but she could not stand to be away from home while her mother and ex-lover might be fighting it out in her apartment. All four of them became shut-ins, and I can only imagine the tension. My mother called them every day, sometimes three-four times a day. Harwinder told her that Mpende cried all the time, even Kunti, that there was nothing in the house to eat, that the boy just lay on his sleeping bag all day, threatening them when they tried to take the child for some exercise. "I do not know who will go mad first," Harwinder said. "Sometimes I think that I will kill him."

"Just what you need in the family," Jill said.

My mother really got upset the day she called and no one picked up the phone. She brooded all day, trying again and again. She called Nitasha. Had they called her? Shawn. Couldn't he go to New Brunswick and see if they were all right?

No one answered the next day either. "They have all disappeared," she said. "He has killed them, all of them, and run away, like these people on TV. We must catch him, put him in the jail, in the electric chair."

I did not want to fly all the way to Newark unless I was sure something devastating had gone wrong. Shawn had taught me that. I called him. "My mother is upset. Just take the train to New Brunswick, take a cab to Kunti's apartment, and knock on the door. I'll reimburse you. I'll pay you for investigating. If no one answers, get the super to open the door. If it's bad, I'll catch the next flight."

"I'm going to London," he said. "I handed in my resignation."

"Shawn," I said, "it's not a resignation until you've worked for a few years. You've just quit, before you could make anything."

"I can't get caught up in this acquisitive, work-until-you-drop culture. Maybe *you* can."

"*I* can?"

What could I do? He had simply not contracted the immigrant disease, even after a year in a Los Angeles high school and four years at Harvard. None of my nieces and nephews had it. But then they'd been sent; they had not immigrated of their own free wills, and for them life back home in the well-to-do families my brothers-in-law had provided for them, even Kanwar when he had been young, had always been more comfortable than being on their own in America. You had to want to escape from the home you were brought up in, had to want to make it on your own, on your own terms, in a better place, to do something for your family, yourself.

Shawn called back late that night, after my mother, even I had gone to bed. "They're gone," he said.

"What do you mean they're gone?"

"Asante came to the door. He thought I had something to do with it. 'Where's my daughter, you dot-headed bastard!' Can you believe that? I've never called him names. 'Where's my cousin?' I said. 'How the fuck would I know?' He threatened me. 'If you don't tell me where she is,' sort of thing. I must have convinced him I don't know—'Why would I come looking for them if I knew where they are?' He calmed down. I must have spent two hours with him. You know, Hari, they're bad. The guy's a wreck. He didn't hit me or anything. Sat down on his sleeping bag and cried. I know he's a lazy bastard and all that, but who are we to say that only rich men can have kids? That to love a kid you have to bust your butt to buy a house in the suburbs, a private school."

"It's called responsibility," I said. "Your parents did it. I—"

"How is he to find out where they went?" Shawn interrupted. "New Brunswick cops just laugh at him. 'Now the whole family is missing,' they say, and they almost care."

But Harwinder, Kunti and the kid were not out of touch for long. Not two hours after Shawn hung up, I got a call from Baby. "Do not worry. They are fine. I put them on a plane."

"A plane? Where are they?"

"They are on their way to Nairobi. I asked them to stay with me, but they would not. In Nairobi, they say, the boy will never follow. He has no money. And they think they can bribe these Kenyans to deny him a visa. Shawn is coming back to London. Did he tell you?"

I woke my mother to comfort her. "It is good," she said. "There he cannot follow. Only how will they get money?"

"Biji, Kunti had no money, even here."

What is it that makes some people ambitious enough to support whole families, to go all the way to that first million, while others cannot pay their bills from one month to the next, such poor decisions do they make? Is it genetic? Is it learned? It could not be a social phenomenon. My nieces and nephews came from the best of families. Maybe something in America had brought the family down. But in America an immigrant is supposed to rise.

"Sleep now," I said. "We'll call Harwinder in the morning."

My mother reported back to me, after she had spoken to Harwinder, that Harwinder did not want to disappear, as her son had disappeared, but she could not possibly have told us where they were going. "They did not know *what* to do. The boy went out. Quickly they got up and took a taxi to the airport. Bags were packed, from that time they tried to come to California. Whole night they were at the airport! They were afraid he would come after them. Then they got a flight to London."

All those years in America, Kunti's American degree, even the lifestyle she seemed to have adopted, more American than Indian, only to go back and live with her mother and paternal grandmother in Nairobi.

"Why did you go?" I asked Harwinder. "You could have gotten a job here. Maybe not a teaching job. You could have worked out visitation with the father."

"I was so afraid of him," she said, "that he would take the only grandchild I might ever have in this life. Even Kunti was afraid of him. She is better now. She will get a job here. Mama is at home to watch the child. I will find a nurse for her. These African ladies are very good with children. We will send her to a very good school. Only you must give us something for the child."

"Certainly," I said.

"Ranjit is here."

"He's there?"

"Astrologer has said. He may be in Africa already, making his way back to Nairobi. Just let him come, and we will send him to you. He can repair cars in your Midas place. No favors! Only the usual wage. He is good with motorcycles. He never wanted to go to college. Just like his father. Everyone says I fell in love with Kanwar. But how could I love him? He was rich. I knew we could not stay in the Middle East. I thought England, India. I never thought he would return to Africa. Even *he* said he had no freedom there. I wanted to study. Did you know that? Jeety said, 'Do not worry. I will pay your fees.' But do you know what happened to the money she earned at the Cottage Industries Emporium? Our father did not approve. He was afraid that if he did not marry us, we would be on his hands for the rest of our lives. But I would not have been on anybody's hands. I would have been a university professor, someone else's wife."

Whenever I see a flyer—missing June 19, 1988; missing, January 5, 1996—I think about my nephew, miserable, cold, starving on the street in some filthy American city. Or stowing away aboard a freighter to Europe or East Asia, just as cold and hungry, drunk on his own sense of freedom. Jill is convinced he's dead—of exposure or an overdose or by the hand of some predator of the same species. The highest rate of death for boys is accidents.

On a Friday night in April I'm sitting at the kitchen table reviewing the forms my accountant has completed. I will have to take a lot of money out for Rosa's college. Mentally adding the net worth of the business to the income it has produced, the house we moved to after the business started bringing in some profits, I see what I am worth, and I guess I should be satisfied. Instead I feel unsettled. I can make a lot more if I advertise, or better yet, scrape together enough to buy another franchise.

Rosa comes home, and I automatically raise my wrist before my eyes. I'm not even wearing my watch, but I know it's early. I can't admit how well she has conditioned me to midnight, some nights even later. She sits across from me. "Taxes?"

I nod.

"Cal is a bargain," she says, "compared to Princeton," where she had always said she wanted to go, especially after we had first arrived, when she missed her friends in Jersey.

"You can go anywhere you want," I say. "Stanford."

"That good?"

"You meet the right kind of people in the Ivy League," I remind her. "Look at Shawn: even in London he's known as an American golden boy."

"Pretty good," she says, "considering that he was born an Indian brown boy."

"English brown boy."

Jill walks in from the family room. "You're home early."

I guess, "Ten o'clock is not exactly early."

"Dad," Rosa says, getting up to put a glass beneath the refrigerator tap.

"Where do you want your graduation party?" Jill asks, "here or in a restaurant? Hotel? The beach?"

"We were going to invite the cousins," Rosa says. "Remember? You think they'll come? Nitasha is the only one still on this continent, and she can't get away in June."

"It's about time at least one of them had a reason not to drop everything and take a vacation," I say.

"Oh, Dad."

"Nitasha's happy," Jill says, sitting down at the table across from me, "though your mother said that even in the joint family in India she had servants doing the kind of work she does in that motel."

I'm amazed at how much Punjabi Jill has come to understand without ever learning how to speak it.

"She'll be happier if Aunt Jeety brings her back an orphan," Rosa says.

"Why are the kids in this family so intent on raising children without the benefits of fathers?" I ask. I eye Rosa suspiciously knowing how impossible it is to avoid sex in this country and remembering how mad I got when Jill told me she had taken our daughter to the pharmacy and bought her condoms.

"The kids in this family are a lot happier than they ever were in this country," Jill says. "Nitasha's got a job, a home, someone to share it with. And if she can adopt, she'll become a mother without having to give up her happiness to put up with a man's family."

"What's that supposed to mean?" I ask.

"She's bashing family," Rosa says. "Mom's always bashing family."

"Do you realize," Jill asks, "how much more peaceful our lives are now that the kids are settled?"

"I wouldn't call Ranjit settled," I say. "I don't know what kind of trouble his sister might be in now either."

"She's working in the national park," Rosa says, "seeing a guy from Australia or something, some kind of scientist."

"How do you know that?" I ask.

"Gossip."

"Nitasha called," Jill confirms. "After Jeety brings your mother back from India, she's flying to Niagara Falls for the summer."

"If she doesn't bring a baby," Rosa says, "'Tasha will get one when she goes to India in January. God, she has the right idea: close up every year and spend the winter in a warm place."

"Shawn is still the real success in the family," I say. "He may be a London banker, but at least he's a banker."

"What about Sheela?" Rosa challenges me. "She's well on her way to being a surgeon, and even in India, that's major."

"Just see to it that you do as well in college," I say.

"Dad," she says, "I got into Berkeley. Will you ease up?"

All of my sisters still talk about coming: Nitasha will buy a motel in San Francisco, and Jeety will come to help her run it. Harwinder will be back, as soon as Ranjit is found. In a few years Kunti will not have to worry about Mpende's father anymore. He will forget about his child. Even Kanwar has forgotten about his children. Mpende is an American citizen. If Kunti did not insist that private schools in Kenya were better than any school she could afford in the United States, she would send Mpende here to live with us. Mpende will definitely come for college. Shawn will be back. With a Harvard degree he can work anywhere in the world. He is only waiting for his father to retire. Then the whole family will live with Shawn in New York. The family is looking for a lady doctor for him. Even Sheela must come back. Why should she be a doctor in India or England when she can make a million in America?

I find myself in full agreement. What can Kunti do, assisting a scientist in Nairobi, that she can't do here? How can Shawn get the experience he needs across an ocean from Wall Street? But I want to tell my sisters: making a million is harder than any of them realizes, even now. It takes ambition. It takes more work than any of them imagine. It takes a craving that cannot be satisfied in any other way. It is a disease. Those who catch it may be trapped in America forever, trying to make enough to satisfy the family, trying to prove that they were right to come, trying to show this country they are just as good, better, than the wealthy men who made America the richest country in the world.

12 Second Generation

Rosa Kaur Gill
Berkeley, California

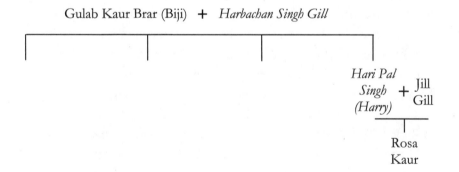

Gulab Kaur Brar (Biji) **+** *Harbachan Singh Gill*

Hari Pal Singh (Harry) **+** Jill Gill

Rosa Kaur

213

D AD SAYS I'm the only second-generation immigrant in what he calls the third generation of the family. All my cousins are first generation like him because they were born in India and England. So I can't see why he calls me an immigrant at all.

"I was born here," I say.

"You could be President," he says. "And that's why you must study. Graduate with honors. Get a job. Not just a job but a career. And when you're old enough, marry someone who has studied just as hard, worked as hard and made a lot of money. You've got to show them. America is not all fun and disrespect. America's a place where you can make your dreams come true."

"My dream is that one day you'll get off my back."

"What kind of talk is that? If I didn't push you, you would not be in Berkeley today."

For a long time I thought I'd go to Princeton, back east. But in the end, I didn't want to go that far from home. Dad says it's a good thing I'm staying on the west coast as long as my cousins don't make it across the country, especially Ranjit, the cousin I have never met. But Dad has always been a little over-protective. When he wasn't workaholic. And I don't think it's right to give up on a person just because he's suffering from an addiction, no matter what he might be addicted to. "Your cousin Ranjit beat up his own father, even his mother," Dad said. "And anyone who hits my sister has to contend with me." That's why Dad's sisters send those strands of colored thread, beaded and tasseled every year. Sometimes Dad manages to tie them—rakhis—on his wrist, and if one of my aunts happens to be visiting in August, he gives her all the cash he has in his wallet. I'm supposed to tie them on my cousins, but I haven't seen Shawn since we moved to California, since *he* did not move back after Harvard, and where would I even send one for Ranjit?

I have never even heard his voice. My grandmother called Kunti to ask why he didn't call when he reached New Jersey, and when

Ranjit got on the phone and asked her for a few hundred bucks, she ragged on him so much that he hung up.

"He went through the money your aunt Baby and Harwinder gave him fast," my father said. "It's got to be more than alcohol."

Seems like everybody in the family is always asking my dad for money. Whenever Nitasha's parents could not get the money out of India, Dad paid her tuition and room and board. After she started working he got really mad when she asked for what she called loans every few months. "If you can't meet your expenses," he told her, "you've got one or two options: either you get a better paying job or you move into a cheaper apartment. Or both. You can get a room-mate." It took Nitasha ten years, but she finally listened. She has a job, hotel management. The room comes free. She even has a room-mate, though everybody, except my dad, thinks they're lesbians. "She's just immature," Dad says, "and she's always been picky. That's why she hasn't found a husband." Her mom's upset that she's living in Canada instead of the United States, but people go where the work is, the university, the company or opportunity; even *I* know that.

When Kunti decided to have her baby, Dad warned her: she would have to struggle if she had a baby before she was established in a job or married to a man who could support a child. "So now you're struggling," he says, "and you want the family to underwrite a mistake that everyone in this family advised you to prevent."

Shawn used to call when his parents wouldn't give him money. Dad would always tell him that he'd have to call Uncle Arora and ask before he could give him anything, and Shawn would withdraw his request. But when Sheela wanted to go to college, Aunt Baby and Uncle Arora expected *us* to pay. Sheela would work part time, the plan was, and put herself through a community college near us. "How will she afford a car?" my dad asked. "We don't have any buses she can take to this minimum-wage job or two-year college. Will her wages also cover her insurance? Gas? Books? Does she have a coat in California? Hat? Gloves? I mean, we'll be glad to have her. We'll give her one of Rosa's coats, all the food she can eat . . ."

The old story is that when our parents were kids they had to walk to school, miles, in the snow and rain. But my dad wasn't even *in* this country until graduate school. *His* story is that he never asked his family for a cent. Every day he checked all of the bulletin boards on campus: *wanted: students to paint apartments, move furniture, participate in scientific experiments.* He says he even stooped so low as to sell his stool to a biology lab. ("Don't you do that," he says. "I'll send you money.") "I would do anything," he says, "and most students in this country would. I paid tuition with that money. My family never had to send anything. And do you know? My sisters never sent a cent."

Mom said she always hoped my cousins would have more sense than the older generation. "But in this country, where there's so much freedom, it's like the first time your grandmother ever saw a supermarket. There was so much to choose from, such variety, she couldn't decide on anything."

Only Ranjit never asked my dad for money. He still might, if he's alive. No one knows what happened to him. Kunti put up his picture in the neighborhood, asked the people on the street. The police listed him as a missing person. Dad hired a detective. He gets pictures from morgues all over the country—dead boys fitting Ranjit's description. He sends them to Shawn because Shawn knew Ranjit better than any of the other cousins. And Dad doesn't believe his sister or Kunti can deal with pictures of the dead, even if they don't turn out to be Ranjit.

Sometimes when I'm daydreaming, walking on the Berkeley campus, through Sather Gate and up Bancroft toward my dorm, I picture myself running into an Indian in his twenties, handsome, like Shawn, with an impeccable English accent, more English than Kunti's, which has faded after almost ten years in this country. We walk together, up into the Berkeley hills, where we can look down on the San Francisco Bay glistening in the sun until the fog rolls in and I get cold, and this guy who calls himself Ron puts his leather jacket around my shoulders. We get to talking but there's something mysterious about him that he won't reveal. In some versions I sleep with him before I find out he's my cousin—too many animated discussions of *Oedipus Rex* in freshman English. (And not enough sex, but don't tell my father!) From what I know about Ranjit he'd be the last man to scratch out the eyes that attract him to forbidden women. In every version of my daydream I deliver him to the family like the part of it that I will never be, with my distance in California, my American childhood and European-American mother. Everyone is suddenly grateful to my Dad—Aunt Harwinder, Kunti. We get Ranjit drinking carrot juice and working out. He is full of the wisdom of the road, like Ulysses or Kerouac. He becomes the brother I never had.

But off the pungent, shoulder-to-shoulder streets of Berkeley, all by myself between four cinder-block walls that cannot be dressed up, even with posters of Keanu Reeves and Tom Cruise, the part of me Dad taught to understand theorems knows that even if Ranjit turns up he will never consider me the sister his mother always said we cousins are. It may be a small world to the family, spread out from the Pacific all the way around to the Atlantic Ocean, but anyone who wants to hide in it can disappear without even trying. So when Mom calls—early one morning before I have to get up—I think for a second that they've matched the dental records Aunt Harwinder brought from Africa. But Mom says, "Rosa? It's your grandmother. A heart attack. In her sleep. Dad found her." And I cry, not for the loss of the grandmother who lived with us—the mother who watched all of her children move away from India to the whole rest of the world. Not for my father, who has done little but think about death in the past few months and will now be blamed for not knowing my grandmother had a weak heart. But for the nephew my father will never find, the son of one of that grandmother's lost daughters, lost himself, the cousin-brother I will never know.